He wanted to see his son—now.

Before he had time to figure out what was bothering him about this woman. He wasn't going to let her— or anyone—stop him. Not now, when he was so close.

"Look," Linc found himself saying, "it's obvious you could use some help around here, and I could use a job for a few days. I'd be willing to work for three meals a day."

"Why... that's unheard of," Jillian sputtered.

Damn her vulnerability. Once again he reminded himself of the reason he was here in the first place.

The air surrounding Jillian suddenly felt heavy. And for the next few moments, she thought about how beautifully masculine he was—and how totally feminine she felt in his presence.

"What is it you really want here, Mr. Rider?"

Dear Reader,

At Silhouette Romance we're celebrating the start of 1994 with a wonderful lineup of exciting love stories. Get set for a year filled with terrific books by the authors you love best, and brand-new names you'll be delighted to discover.

Those FABULOUS FATHERS continue, with Linc Rider in Kristin Morgan's *Rebel Dad*. Linc was a mysterious drifter who entered the lives of widowed Jillian Fontenot and her adopted son. Little did Jillian know he was a father in search of a child—*her* child.

Pepper Adams is back with *Lady Willpower*. In this charming battle of wills, Mayor Joe Morgan meets his match when Rachel Fox comes to his town and changes it—and Joe!

It's a story of love lost and found in Marie Ferrarella's *Aunt Connie's Wedding*. Carole Anne Wellsley was home for her aunt's wedding, and Dr. Jefferson Drumm wasn't letting her get away again!

And don't miss Rebecca Daniels's *Loving the Enemy*. This popular Intimate Moments author brings her special brand of passion to the Silhouette Romance line. Rounding out the month, look for books by Geeta Kingsley and Jude Randal.

We hope that you'll be joining us in the coming months for books by Diana Palmer, Elizabeth August, Suzanne Carey and many more of your favorite authors.

Anne Canadeo
Senior Editor

Please address questions and book requests to:
Reader Service
U.S.: P.O. Box 1325, Buffalo, NY 14269
Canadian: P.O. Box 1050, Niagara Falls, Ont. L2E 7G7

REBEL DAD
Kristin Morgan

Silhouette
ROMANCE™
Published by Silhouette Books
America's Publisher of Contemporary Romance

To my own "rebel,"
who's found his way home—at last.
And to my son, Lance.

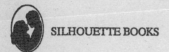 SILHOUETTE BOOKS

ISBN 0-373-08982-1

REBEL DAD

Copyright © 1994 by Barbara Lantier Veillon

Printed in U.S.A.

KRISTIN MORGAN

lives in Lafayette, Louisiana, the very heart of Acadiana, where the French language of her ancestors is still spoken fluently by her parents and grandparents. Happily married to her high school sweetheart, she has three children. She and her husband have traveled all over the South, as well as other areas of the United States and Mexico, and they both count themselves lucky that their favorite city, New Orleans, is only two hours away from Lafayette.

In addition to her writing, she enjoys cooking and preparing authentic Cajun foods for her family with recipes passed on to her through the generations. Her hobbies include reading—of course!—flower gardening and fishing. She loves walking in the rain, newborn babies, all kinds of music, chocolate desserts and love stories with happy endings. A true romantic at heart, she believes all things are possible with love.

Linc Rider On Fatherhood...

If asked, I would've said that fatherhood wasn't for a guy like me.

I mean, I was a kid from the streets. I lived by a whole other set of rules than most folks. I didn't know the first thing about being a parent. A wife and kids? Uh-uh. No way.

Then I discovered that I had this eleven-year-old kid somewhere in the world. And *wham*... from that moment on I was possessed with this need to find him. After all, he was mine. We shared the same blood. We belonged together.

Boy, was I ever in for a rude awakening. I soon learned that being a good father meant a heck of a lot more than just passing on my genes. It meant caring—a lot. It meant putting my kid's needs before my own. It meant being there for him every second of every day, no matter how I felt. I learned all that by watching my kid's adoptive mother, Jillian Fontenot. She's incredible, beautiful and warm. And the best mom any kid could ask for. She really loves Eric.

Which truly spells trouble for me, because I've decided that my freedom is something I can do without. What I *can't* do without is my son; I've lost enough time with him as it is. But can I risk breaking Jillian's heart by tearing them apart?

Chapter One

He had a son.

Even after two months, the shocking discovery was still brand-new to Linc Rider and it caused his chest to squeeze tight with emotion.

Never mind that it had taken a chance meeting with the mother of Trixie Mcguire, a girl he'd known from his old neighborhood, for him to finally be told that Trixie had given birth to his child while he was away in the army and had given him up for adoption to some so-called *good* family from Louisiana. A quick inventory of his life had told him that his kid was the only worthwhile accomplishment he had to show for his thirty years of existence. The boy was his. They belonged together. No one had the right to keep them apart. No one.

It was destiny, pure and simple. How else could he explain meeting up with Trixie's mother after all these years and being told he was a father? Certainly, he wouldn't have ever guessed that his one-time mistake with Trixie Mcguire had resulted in her getting pregnant. She'd been the one to follow him to New Orleans with the intention of seducing *him*. He hadn't even been aware of her purpose in coming to Louisiana to find him until that morning when he'd awakened to discover her in his bed. Only then had she decided to tell him how she'd purposely gotten him drunk the night before so she could dupe him into sleeping with her. Her motive, according to what she'd said, had been to get even with her boyfriend, who had just dumped her for her best friend. She had wanted to use Linc in her plan for revenge because he and her ex-boyfriend had been buddies back in high school. Linc could still recall how much he'd hated her in that moment.

But today, even that didn't matter anymore. Only one thing did. His son.

Undoubtedly, Trixie's mother now knew she had made a big mistake in thinking that after twelve years he wouldn't care anymore, one way or the other. Hell, he would've cared when it happened. But no one, least of all Trixie, had bothered to inform him that he was going to be a father.

He knew he had a battle ahead of him. Why, even the damned legal system wasn't on his side. In fact, two attorneys whom he had consulted had already turned him down as a client, telling him that they didn't think he stood a fat chance in hell of proving the boy was his. Another attorney had said he'd take the case, but doubted if anything would come of it. In reality, the only shred of proof he had that he was the boy's father at all was old lady Mcguire's word. And now, she was denying everything she'd told him. It seemed that Trixie had convinced her mother once more that it was best for everyone concerned to leave the past alone. Period.

Well, maybe it was best for Trixie and her new city-councilman husband. But not for him. So maybe twelve years ago he wouldn't have taken his responsibility as seriously as now. Hell, back then he was nothing more than a confused kid from the streets himself. He'd had nothing going for him that summer day when, on a sudden whim that had more to do with his being angry with himself and Trixie Mcguire than anything else, he'd strolled into an army recruiting station and signed up with Uncle Sam. Still, if he'd known about the baby, he would have tried to do something to help out. If there was one thing he had to believe about himself, it was that, even at his worst, Linc Rider wasn't anything like the sorry bastard who had left his six-teen-year-old mother alone and pregnant, without any place to turn to for help. For one thing, *he* wanted his son.

And that was what made the report he'd gotten last night from the detective he'd hired to find the boy so rewarding. The investigator, using the small bit of information that Linc had given him, had discovered that his kid was living in Pine Creek, Louisiana, with his adoptive mother and grandmother. The detective had also learned that the boy's adoptive fifty-one-year-old father had died from a heart attack three years earlier. The mother, now thirty-four, ran her deceased husband's mercantile store, along with her aging mother-in-law. The trouble was, according to Linc's way of thinking, the woman didn't have one single incentive to allow him to become a part of his son's life. Not a one.

That was why he had a plan.

And the setup in Pine Creek couldn't have been better for what he intended. The two women were like sitting ducks, waiting for his kill. Winning his son away from them was going to be easier than he thought.

His scheme was simple. Somehow he would infiltrate their world, and befriend his son. Then, when the time was right, he'd tell his kid the truth and get the boy to go away with him. Together they would forge a father-and-son relationship that could never be severed.

He'd be a damned good father, too. He'd be there for the boy through thick and thin. He might not have a college degree to his credit, but so far he'd done okay for himself. He'd learned a lot while in the army, including auto mechanics, and today he had the reputation of being one of the finest auto technicians in the state of Mississippi. Maybe even in the whole South. He could fix any kind of engine, computerized or not, foreign or domestic. It would be easy for him to get a job with one of the big dealerships in either Biloxi or Mobile.

Better yet, he could use the money he'd managed to save up over the years as a down payment on a mechanic's shop in some small town. There he could purchase a nice, comfortable house in a nice, comfortable neighborhood that had lots of shade trees in the backyard. God knew, the last thing he wanted for his boy was the kind of street-smart education in life that he'd gotten.

But first things first. For now, just getting past the anxiety of meeting his son for the first time was enough. For the most part, though, he wasn't all that worried about his son's reaction to him. Only every now and then did a small blade of fear cut through him. And only for a fleeting moment. Whenever he felt the sharp pain, he always reminded himself that, just as he had as a kid, his son was probably yearning to know his father. Linc could still recall the many times he had sat on the steps of the decaying building where he and his mother lived, and daydreamed about his old man suddenly showing up in their lives, saying he cared about them. But, of course, that never happened. Nor would it ever. Linc had long ago realized that the old man who had fathered him couldn't have cared less about what had happened to him and his mother. Actually, no one had cared.

Not even his mother's parents, who thought themselves too righteous to love their illegitimate grandchild. So, in the end, his mother had turned to prostitution as a means of supporting them. Linc would never forgive his so-called father—or his grandparents, for that matter—for what they'd done—especially to his mother. But while he might have hated the world from which he came, he knew it had made him the man he was today...cunning...ruthless... determined.

Heaven help him, though, he didn't necessarily want all those same qualities instilled in his son. He just wanted his kid to grow up...normal. He wanted the boy to understand that his being given up for adoption wasn't his fault. That there was nothing wrong with him. Linc had lived all his life with the tormenting pain of rejection. If there was any way he could prevent his son from experiencing that kind of suffering, he was determined to do it.

Gazing around the small kitchen where he stood, Linc recalled that he had often been told he had a way with women. Well, his attitude toward them was really quite simple. He could either take 'em or leave 'em, depending on the circumstances, but one thing was for sure. Charming the pants off his kid's adoptive, country-bumpkin mother was going to be a cinch for someone of his caliber. And if that was what it would take to get his boy back, then he would do it—and he would do it without feeling in the least bit guilty.

Packing to leave for Pine Creek took the same amount of time it did for him to gobble down a stale doughnut and a cup of black, lukewarm coffee. Only an army green duffel bag stuffed with his clothes, one used blanket, and a small framed snapshot of him and his mother when he was seven years old and she was still a beautiful woman was worth taking along. Everything else in the clean, though sparsely furnished, two-room apartment he rented by the week belonged to the landlord.

By tonight, he would have seen his son for the first time. That alone in this world was the most important thing.

It was just another hot, uneventful day in early June, according to Jillian Fontenot. Each time a customer opened the door to Fontenot's Grocery and Market, a tan, gritty mist from the graveled parking lot out front floated in and settled on the different sizes and types of grocery items that lined the long, white-painted shelves. The air-conditioning unit in the window behind her was pumping out air as hard as a weekend jogger. The problem was, it pumped up the electric bill, as well.

Jillian sat on the edge of the wooden stool behind the checkout counter and sighed heavily. She felt exhausted from the long day, the summer's heat, and from the nagging fear that no matter how hard she tried to keep her head above water, she was fooling herself. Worse, she knew that if she *did* go under, she would take along with her the future of the one person in the whole world who meant more to her than life itself. Her brave, eleven-year-old son Eric.

Suddenly realizing the negativity of her thoughts, Jillian straightened her shoulders. By golly, she wasn't a quitter. She had gumption. And plenty of it. She *was not* going to give in to her fear of failure. Not now. Not ever. A brighter day was just beyond the next horizon for herself—and for Eric, too. She'd make sure of it. After all, on the day that she and her deceased husband Henry had driven to Biloxi to pick up their ten-day-old son and to sign the necessary adoption papers for Eric to become their own, she'd made a promise to herself that she'd always be there for her son, no matter what. Maybe fate hadn't allowed her to give birth to him, but it had allowed her the wonderful opportunity to give him love and stability, and plenty of it.

No, she wasn't going to give up because of their financial problems. She had her son, and she had her health. She could, and would, get the family business back on its feet. Maybe even more so than before the oil crash of the mid-eighties. It would just take time for their small country store to make a comeback from all the losses it had incurred when so many of their customers had lost their jobs and were unable to pay back the credit Henry had extended to them over the years.

Besides, Jillian thought, in spite of all the hardships, hadn't she kept the store from bankruptcy? And if she were completely honest with herself, didn't she know deep down inside that even if Henry *had* lived, even with all his years of experience, he couldn't have done any better a job of it than she had? She had reason to be proud of herself—and for the most part, she was. For the first time in her life she was earning her own way in this world, and there wasn't one darn reason for her to think she couldn't continue.

"Jillian?" came the aging voice from across the store.

Her mother-in-law, affectionately called Gram by all those who knew her, had turned eighty-two a month ago. Today the older woman's arthritis was extremely painful when she tried to walk and so she'd spent most of the afternoon in bed. "Did I take my afternoon dose of medicine?"

"Yes, Gram. At four o'clock," Jillian replied with a shake of her head. Her mother-in-law was so forgetful these days. Ever since Henry's death, her health had steadily declined. "I'll give it to you again before bedtime."

"Don't forget," Gram said before closing the door that separated the front part of the building that housed the market from the rear that was their residence. The living quarters consisted of three small bedrooms, one bath and a

kitchen-and-sitting-room combination that was neither
modern nor convenient. Often times, after closing for the
day, Jillian had to wait her turn for a hot, soothing bath.
Often times, there simply wasn't enough hot water to go
around.

And oftentimes, while lying alone in her bed, Jillian felt
the walls closing in on her and wished her life had been different, with the exception of Eric, of course. But then she
would feel guilty. This store belonged to her husband's
family. They had taken her in when she had no place else to
go after her grandmother's death. Henry, though twenty
years older than she, had married her and given her the security she had needed. And while he'd had his own per-
sonal reasons for wanting a wife who was young and strong
and capable of working from sunup to sundown, he'd been
more than good to her. And the proof of that was Eric.
When she'd asked him to adopt his distant cousin's baby,
he'd agreed without hesitation.

And maybe he'd had his reasons for that, too. Their
marriage hadn't been an intimate one. Not even in the beginning. Maybe if she hadn't been so young and naive,
maybe if she had known him better and felt more at ease,
she could have found the nerve to question him about his
lack of desire for her. But as it turned out, she'd hidden her
bewilderment until she'd convinced herself that his rejection no longer mattered to her. Somehow, though, she'd always known that his agreeing to adopt Eric was his way of
making peace with her.

But that part of her life was behind her now and she
wasn't the same naive little girl whom Henry had married all
those years ago. She'd grown up in spite of the emotional
neglect she'd suffered during her marriage, and today she
had her own ideas about romantic love. To her way of
thinking, it simply didn't exist. Not in real life, anyway. Not

for ordinary people. Couples who came together did so as a matter of survival.

She wasn't alone in her way of thinking. Most folks around Pine Creek thought as she did. Like her, they knew what really counted in life—what was really needed—and, for the most part, they didn't go around falling all over themselves in the name of love. And the few who did were considered fools.

She knew, therefore, that the ridiculous dreams she'd been having lately were just that—ridiculous. Childish. A product of too much late-night television when she should have been sleeping. How could she even think about herself and some James Dean look-alike doing it on the checkout counter in the grocery store? In broad daylight, mind you. With both of them naked. Why, if ever—and even that was a big if—she chose to have a man in her life, undoubtedly he would have to be a hardworking, dependable soul, with the backbone of a mule. His sexual appetite would be of little concern to her. Reliability. That was what counted most. Someone capable of taking responsibility with a serious grip.

Right?

Right.

But she had nothing to worry about. Because what kind of man in his right mind would take on a widow, her eleven-year-old son, her aging mother-in-law and her few measly hopes for their failing family business? He would have to be out of his mind, or desperate—or both—and she certainly didn't want a man like that hanging around. She was surviving just fine alone.

Jillian pulled her thoughts back into the present and heard the sound of a vehicle as it came to a stop near the front of the store. From where she sat behind the counter, it sounded like a motorcycle, but she couldn't be sure. She glanced at the clock on the wall and saw it was twenty minutes before seven. Twenty minutes before closing time. Just another late shopper, she figured.

Then she decided that if it was indeed a motorcycle she had heard, it was probably her neighbor, Barney Langford. For the past week he had been stopping in each day at this time to buy a six-pack of beer. Last night he'd lingered for the longest time and Jillian had gotten the feeling he'd wanted to ask her something. But she'd been too busy with a couple of last-minute shoppers and he'd never gotten around to it. For some reason, she felt relieved about that. According to local gossip, he and his live-in girlfriend had just split up and he was looking for someone new. But at age forty, Barney still drank beer as though he thought it would go out of style any moment and chased after women in similar fashion. Everyone in the area knew that he never held a steady job any longer than a couple of months at a time. He liked to brag about the fact that he hadn't seen the inside of a church in years. According to Gram, who always kept up with such things, his poor mama prayed for him daily. For those reasons alone Jillian wouldn't have ever considered going out with him. But more important was the fact that her son was at an impressionable age. And to her way of thinking, the likes of Barney Langford was a far cry from the type of man she wanted influencing him.

But when the entrance door was opened, one glance told Jillian that it wasn't Barney who had entered. The guy she saw was much younger, much taller and much better looking than her pesky neighbor, and she was quick to realize that it wasn't every day the likes of such a man happened through her store. Automatically, she found herself sitting up straight and tightening her stomach muscles.

His piercing blue eyes met Jillian's and a sudden feeling of danger oozed through her, causing her breath to catch in her throat. When she lifted her hand to sweep back her hair from her face, it shook.

Surely the man meant her no harm, she told herself. Why, he wasn't even carrying a gun—or a knife. At least, not that she could see. Crime, she reminded herself, was practically unheard of in these parts. Surely she had nothing to fear from him.

The stranger wore tight, faded jeans and a white T-shirt, the kind that Henry had worn as underwear during the damp, cold winters that often plagued south Louisiana. The kind her imaginary James Dean look-alike would have been wearing in her daydream, if he'd had any clothes on at all, that is. This guy had ink black hair and eyes as blue as the sky. He was gazing directly at her and she gave a fleeting thought to what she could possibly have in her store that he could possibly want, which didn't make any sense, and she knew it.

He looked to be near her age—possibly a few years her junior—and he reminded her of a character from one of those soap operas that her mother-in-law watched faithfully. He was incredibly sexy, and something pulled hard and deep inside her as he stood there, staring at her over the counter as if he was sizing her up for the kill. Suddenly she felt herself go hot all over and knew without a doubt that her insides had just ignited into a slow, easy burn.

Did she look as if she were on fire?

Now that the interstate highway had come through just ten miles down the road, strangers didn't pass through Pine Creek all that often anymore, which, of course, didn't help business any. In this case, though, Jillian was positive she'd never seen this man before, because he wasn't the kind easily forgotten. And besides, she knew it was unlikely that she could have come away from a previous encounter with him without having some kind of scar to show for it.

She felt sizzling hot...feverish, she told herself as she pressed the palm of her hand to her forehead and then to her cheek, though in reality, she knew such an ill condition was highly unlikely. She had never been sick a day in her life. Still, maybe last year's winter flu virus that had put hundreds to bed in the area had finally gotten the better of her immune system. It was possible, wasn't it?

"Can I help you?" she heard herself asking, though it was more from habit than from anything else. Apparently, if working at all, her brain had switched to low power.

She slipped off the stool and stood with her hands folded and resting on the counter for added support. Then she glanced down and saw that her skin was chafed and her nails broken from the many long hours of hard work that it took her to manage the store practically single-handedly. She quickly dropped her hands to her sides. Her legs felt weak, as though she had been sitting on them much too long.

"Yeah, maybe you can. Are you the owner?"

"Uh, I...yes, I am," Jillian replied. After all, she did make the necessary decisions concerning the welfare of the business. Besides, any other explanation would have been too lengthy—and far too complicated. By the time she got to the end, he'd have been long gone. She had a feeling he was the type that never stayed put anywhere for very long.

"Well, I was wondering if you were needing any extra help around the place? I'm looking for temporary work," he drawled in a deep, vibrating voice. He stepped up to the counter as his gaze quickly swept across the room. Then he swung his blue eyes to her face and Jillian knew that during his split-second inspection he had noticed every flaw in the place, from the peeling paint high on the walls to the broken shelves to the patched-up windowpanes. Blood gushed to her cheeks, tinting them a deep rose. It wasn't easy for her to accept the deterioration of the store. But there simply wasn't enough money to hire someone to do repairs. At least, not yet. And by the time she closed up the store each day, she usually had other things to do—like supper and laundry and helping Eric with his homework. For now, she was doing the best she could.

Slowly she became aware that the stranger was now giving her another of his split-second inspections, and again she felt he saw every flaw. Growing anxious under his scrutiny, she pushed at her hair, which continually fell across her forehead. Now why hadn't she bothered to put on makeup this morning? And why had she worn the oldest blouse in her closet? Good grief, but she must look a sight.

"Uh, I—I'm sorry. But I'm not hiring."

He glanced around the room again, only this time at a much slower pace. Then, lifting his eyes to the ceiling, he hooked his thumbs into the front pockets of his jeans and shifted his weight to one leg. "Looks to me like you've got some major leaks in your roof."

After gazing at him a moment longer than necessary—it was just that his skin was so deeply tanned, his nose so straight, his eyes so stunningly blue—her gaze followed his and she saw the brown-edged water rings spotting the ceiling. "Yes—I know. It's been leaking for months now."

His gaze fell to her face and she was immediately mesmerized. "It sure looks to me like you could use some help around here."

Jillian sucked in a deep breath. "Well, for your information, needing help and hiring it are two different matters. I can't afford any extra help right now."

"How do you know? I haven't told you my price yet."

Jillian couldn't breath. For some reason, coming from him, the statement sounded ... well ... suggestive. Her legs became even more unsteady than they were earlier. "Look, Mr...."

"Rider. Linc Rider."

"Look, Mr. Rider, nobody works for free and that's the only kind of labor I can afford right now."

"Why don't you call me Linc, okay? Either that, or Easy." He grinned when her eyes widened a degree. "It's just a nickname. Like 'Easy' Rider."

"Oh, I see." Which of course she didn't. But it seemed to make perfect sense to him, so why should she care? He'd be on his way soon. That thought forced a quiver of...what?— disappointment?—to roll across her stomach. Then the telephone rang and she excused herself to answer it.

Linc took the time allotted him to study his enemy. So, this was the woman who stood in the way of having his son. Well, she didn't look so tough to him. In fact, she looked tired. And worried. And just about as vulnerable as a soul could get.

Well, it didn't matter what she looked like, he reminded himself. Because up against him, she didn't stand a hell's chance of winning in the first place. Undoubtedly she didn't know a damned thing about surviving. Not like he did. From the looks of her, she probably had the nature of a pedigree puppy, and that simply wasn't good enough. Because when it came to surviving, Linc knew he could fight like a junkyard dog. And, if need be, he would. Soon he'd have his son by his side. Soon he'd be able to make up for all the lost years.

So where was his kid, anyway? Linc wondered impatiently, looking past the one person who would have wanted to stop him if she'd only known his intentions. He'd been waiting two whole months for this moment. *Correction*— he'd been waiting a lifetime. "Look, lady," Linc found himself saying, "it's obvious you could use some help around here and I could sure use a job for a few days. I'd be willing to work for three meals a day."

"Why...that's unheard of," Jillian sputtered, her eyes swinging up to meet his, causing his stomach to ball up in knots.

Damn the vulnerability he saw in the depths of her wide brown eyes. He tightened his jaw. Her problems weren't his. And the very fact that he had to remind himself of that almost angered him.

Okay. Enough of this small talk. And enough of her, too. He wanted to see his son—*now*. Before his next breath. Before he had time to figure out what was bothering him about this woman. Dammit, he wasn't going to let her—or anyone—stop him. Not now, when he was so close. Once again reminding himself of the reason he was here in the first place, he tilted his head to one side and gave Jillian Fontenot one of his best I-bet-I-can-win-you-over-to-my-side grins. "Really? Do you think I'm asking for too much?"

Jillian's stomach seemed to decompress. He had one gorgeous smile, all right. "Of course not. But where would you stay? Rooms for rent cost money. And anyway, there aren't any around here. At least, not that I know of."

He tucked his fingertips into his back pockets and continued grinning. "That's easy. I could sleep on a blanket under the stars. A person can still do that, you know."

Jillian shrugged. "Yeah, I guess you're right about that. It's a free country."

"No," he said, slowly shaking his head as he gazed at her with eyes so blue she could easily have drowned in them. "Take it from me. Nothing in life is ever free. In the end, the piper always demands payment."

The air surrounding Jillian suddenly felt heavy. For the next few moments, she forgot about all else and just thought about how beautifully masculine he was—and how totally feminine she was feeling in his presence.

But finally she had to admit that she agreed with him. Nothing was free. And no one worked for nothing in this day and age. He had to want something more than three meals a day. And though she couldn't afford to hire him at any price, she was curious as to what he thought his services as a handyman were worth. Or maybe she simply wasn't quite ready for their conversation to end and for him to be on his way. "I agree with what you just said. Which brings me to the next question. What is it that you really want here, Mr. Rider?"

Chapter Two

His blue eyes bored into hers for the longest time. Then suddenly, as though he'd attained some kind of understanding of what she meant, he smiled. "Well, that depends."

Jillian frowned. "On what?"

"McDonald's."

"McDonald's?"

"Yeah. Is there one around here? I could use a burger about now."

"Uh...no."

"See? Just as I thought. Then I've got a problem."

"What problem?" she said, wondering if her questions were beginning to sound as dumb to him as they did to her.

"I've only been in the area a couple of hours and I'm already hungry."

"Look, I'm really sorry that you've got a problem. But your eating habits are not my concern."

"No, but the leaks in your roof sure are."

"Good point," Jillian said, shaking her head in agreement.

"You're darn right they are," he said, doing the same as she was and looking quite pleased with himself.

"But the leaks are *my* concern. *Not* yours," she insisted. Honestly, she didn't know what to make of this guy. She wished she could find it in herself to laugh at his absurd offer, but she couldn't. "It's just that your offer to work for three meals a day doesn't make any sense."

He shrugged. "Look, I'm only in the area because I dropped by unexpectedly to see a friend of mine about a business opportunity he might be interested in. But he's in Florida for a few days. So I thought I'd stick around until he returns. Maybe you know him? His name's Hal Davis."

Jillian shook her head. "No."

"I guess he lives about ten miles from here."

Jillian continued shaking her head. "I know a lot of folks in the area, but I don't recall ever hearing that particular name."

"Maybe your husband knows him."

"I'm widowed."

"Oh, I see," he replied. "That's gotta be tough. I mean, running this place all alone."

"My son helps me," she replied.

Linc felt his stomach sink to the floor. Just the mention of his son—*his* son—caused adrenaline to flood his veins. He was so close. So very close.

He gathered his wits quickly, looked over at Jillian and shrugged. "Well, as I was saying, Hal and I were in the army together a few years ago. He did me a big favor once, and now that I have the means, I'd like to pay him back. I'd have hung around his place, but his wife didn't seem to be too keen on the idea when I suggested it. So I thought about finding temporary work nearby. Something to keep me busy during the next few days, until he comes back."

"Well, maybe someplace else around here needs help. There's a cattle ranch about four miles away. They're always hiring. And I've heard the money's pretty good."

"See, ma'am, you just don't understand. In this case, money isn't a top priority with me. In fact, money could be a problem. If you're paying me, then you expect me to stay until the job you've hired me to do is finished. But if I'm working for nothing—or for three square meals a day," he added with a sexy smile that had undoubtedly convinced every girl he had ever known that he was the answer to her nightly prayers, "then when the sun sets each day, I consider you and me even. And when Hal returns home, I'll be history. That's a promise."

Easy Rider. It described him to a tee. "Is that how you got your nickname, always on the move?" Jillian asked, immediately wondering when and where she'd acquired so much nerve. She felt her face grow warm. For goodness' sake, what business was it of hers how he'd gotten his nickname?

One side of his mouth slid up, changing his sexy smile into a boyish grin, and one side of Jillian's heart flipped over with it. The reaction itself was enough to make her realize that she needed to be exceptionally wary of this man, or she just might end up paying dearly for every single moment she spent in his company.

"Partly," he replied.

She barely registered his reply. She was too busy wondering whether she was going to listen to her own warning. But, oh, no. Not this time. Instead she found herself grinning right back at him, despite a feeling of disappointment in herself. Gracious, but she didn't even know this man, and yet here she was, flirting with him. What would her mother-

in-law or the other women from their church think if they
saw her acting so giddy with a complete stranger? Her smile
vanished as quickly as it came. "Well, I'm sorry, but I
wouldn't think of hiring someone unless I could pay them.
And I can't. Now, please, you'll have to go. I need to close
up for the night."

Linc stood there, gazing at her silently. Finally, he shook
his head in frustration. He hadn't expected this. Anyone else
would have jumped at the offer he'd made. What could he
do to change her mind? Insist she hire him? Yeah ... that
would undoubtedly go over real big with her.

He'd have to think of something else.

"Okay, lady, you win," he said, turning around and
walking toward the front entrance.

From the parking lot out front Jillian heard the sound of
a car door being slammed shut. A second later the entrance
door swung open and her son came rushing inside. He appeared not to notice Linc Rider, who had quickly stepped
out of his path to keep them from colliding.

"What the heck—" Linc retorted.

"Mom! Mom!"

"Now, Eric," Jillian began. "What have I told you about
running in here like that? It's not very polite."

"I know. I'm sorry," he said breathlessly as he rounded
the corner of the checkout counter. "But you're not gonna
believe what happened, Mom." He handed her a printed
sheet of paper that she knew was his report card.

Jillian couldn't help but smile. For a moment she'd forgotten that today was the last day of school. The only reason he was so late in getting home was that he had stayed
after class for baseball practice. Thank goodness a neighbor whose son played on Eric's team was kind enough to
bring him home each day. Otherwise, it would have been a

big problem if she'd had to be the one to pick him up after every practice.

"Look, Mom, all *A*s and *B*s."

"Oh, honey," Jillian replied, giving him a quick hug. "I'm so proud of you." She took the report card from him and literally beamed with pride as she read it. "But what made you think I wouldn't believe your good grades?"

He shook his head. "That's not what I was talking about." Then his grin widened. "Guess what?" he said, standing so straight he almost looked as though he were at attention. Only the pleased look on his face gave away the fact that a drill sergeant wasn't nearby.

"What, honey?"

"What's the best thing that could happen to a guy like me?" he asked, straightening his shoulders even more as a cocky expression settled on his face.

"Well, I don't know," Jillian said, feeling her own excitement building up right along with his. "Did you win this year's history medal at school?"

Eric's frown clearly stated that he was disappointed in what she might have thought would have been the best thing to happen to him. "No, not that. Now guess again. And this time, think harder."

Jillian tried. At least ten things raced through her mind, but not one of them stuck out any more than the others. She knew that lately he and his best friend Wally had made the discovery that girls weren't useless creatures, after all. Still...

"I don't know, Eric. What's the best thing that can happen to an eleven-year-old boy?"

"Well," he said, clearing his throat in the way that adults in authority often do when wanting to command the attention of others, "here goes. I made the all-star team this year. I'm gonna play right field."

"Oh, honey, that's wonderful," Jillian exclaimed.

"And the first tournament is this weekend. We have a bye for our first game. So our next game won't be until that afternoon. I can be there, huh, Mom?"

Nervously, Jillian began wiping her hands down the sides of the blue-jean skirt she wore. "Oh, Eric, I don't know about this weekend. You were supposed to help me patch up the roof on the smokehouse out back, remember?"

From the look on her son's face, Jillian knew she had just smashed his world to smithereens. She saw when his shoulders slumped and the cocky look he'd had on his face quickly disappeared. Tears sprang to his eyes. "I forgot all about that, Mom."

Jillian felt pressure building in her temples. All of Eric's friends had probably made the all-star team. They always did. But this was Eric's first year. How could she stop him from playing in that tournament? What kind of childhood memories would he have when he grew up if she allowed her adult problems to interfere with his fun?

During the past few minutes, she had forgotten that they weren't alone. That the stranger who was on his way out when Eric had arrived had halted his departure and was standing stone still just ten feet away. Suddenly remembering, she glanced back at him and found his blue eyes fixed on them. Every cell in her body felt electrified. "Uh, Mr. Rider, I thought you'd gone."

He didn't bother answering, but the slight surprise in her voice was enough to get Eric's attention and he looked up. "Who's he?"

"He's just someone looking for work," Jillian replied, her tone of voice clearly dismissing Linc as unimportant. "But I've already told him we're not hiring."

"But I heard when you told Gram last night that you could use some help," Eric chimed in as though he were doing her a favor.

"I was just tired last night," Jillian said, defend
self. Why was it that children never heard what you wanted
them to hear and always heard what you didn't?

Besides, she didn't owe anyone an explanation for the way
she felt at certain times. Least of all this stranger.

Eric hung his head. "I know I was supposed to help out
on Saturday, but I didn't think I'd make the all-star team.
But now—"

"Don't worry about it, Eric. We'll fix the smokehouse
some other time. Just keep practicing, okay? Now hurry up
and see about Gram. She isn't feeling very well today. I'll be
in to fix supper real soon."

Eric's face brightened. With an elated grin, he slung his
baseball cleats over his left shoulder and headed for the rear.
He turned back only once. "What's for supper?"

"'Dogs and chili," Jillian replied.

"All right," he said, hurrying off to brag to his grandmother about his latest accomplishments.

For Linc, the past few moments had been incredible.

Control. That was what he needed to concentrate on.
Complete control. So, okay, the kid was his son. His own
flesh and blood. He couldn't think about that for now. He
needed to be tough. Actually, tougher than tough. Later
tonight he could deal with all the raw emotions that were
racing through his body. But not now, when Jillian Fontenot was watching his every move. "Nice-looking kid," he
said, keeping his voice casual.

"I happen to think so," Jillian replied.

"Now, about that job—"

"Like I said, Mr. Rider. There *is* no job. I'm sorry."

Narrowing his eyes, he placed his hands on his hips.
"What is it about me that you don't like?"

Jillian couldn't believe this guy. Boy, did he ever have
some nerve. Still, ignoring the weakness in her knees, she

knew she had to stand her ground. "Nothing. I don't even know you. Now, I think you'd better leave."

"Fine. Suit yourself," Linc replied, keeping a tight rein on his expression and hoping his voice didn't give away any of the anger he was feeling. Damn her, anyway. She was one hardheaded woman. Apparently she wasn't going to be as easy to sway to his side as he'd thought. Without knowing what else to say or do, he once again started for the door.

Watching him, Jillian breathed a sigh of relief. There was something about the man that made her feel . . . well . . . breathless . . . and almost shaken. She felt the sooner he was on his way, the sooner she would feel normal again.

Hopefully.

Just then she heard another motorcycle pulling into the parking lot and this time she had little doubt as to its driver. Within seconds, Barney Langford strolled inside. "Well, if it ain't my little honey bun," he said in an unusually loud voice as he spotted Jillian behind the counter. "Now, how's my favorite gal doing today?" In the next breath, and before Jillian could answer him, he belched.

Jillian rolled her eyes upward. Great. Just great. That was all she needed. A drunken Barney Langford. "You're too late to buy beer, Barney. I've already closed up for the night. Sorry."

He halted in his tracks and glared at her. "It don't look to me like you've closed up." Pointing his finger toward Linc Rider, he snorted and said, "Who's he, the milkman?"

"Barney, now that's enough. Go on home and go to bed," Jillian said in a chastising voice. She wanted to add *and sleep off the booze,* but didn't. At this point she knew antagonizing the inebriated man wasn't going to get him to cooperate with her advice.

But instead of taking the hint, Barney sauntered up to the counter where Linc Rider stood and looked up into the younger man's face as though he was going to challenge him to a duel. "You trying to beat my time, buddy?"

Shocked speechless, Jillian's mouth dropped open. Why that darn Barney Langford! Of all the nerve! Of all the stupidity! Oh, for heaven's sake, why is this happening to me? she wondered.

Linc "Easy" Rider's lips curved into a slight smile and he looked down at Barney in fleeting amusement. "That depends on what you're talking about."

Barney glanced at Jillian with a look in his narrowed gaze that said he thought he had every right to every single ounce of her. "Jillian, you been seeing this guy behind my back?"

"Oh, for crying out loud, Barney," Jillian snapped. "I've had enough. Now I'm warning you, if you don't get out of here, I'm going to call the sheriff."

For a brief moment, her fool neighbor had the audacity to look hurt. But then anger began to seep into his face. "You think you can throw old Barn in the slammer so you can get it on with this guy behind my back? Well, think again. No dame two-times Barney Langford." He began to hiccup.

Even from where she stood, his breath smelled like stale beer. His face was flushed and beaded with sweat as he began to poke Linc Rider in the chest with his index finger. "She's already taken, buddy."

By this time, Jillian had had more than enough. And so, she figured, had Linc Rider. She now realized that Barney was going to be an eventual major problem for her if she didn't do something more to discourage him. Good grief, she didn't need this. Not one darn bit.

She took a deep, deciding breath and came around the counter to stand next to the blue-eyed stranger, who, as of yet, hadn't said more than a couple of words in his defense. But his eyes were narrowed and his jaw was firmly set, telling Jillian that he was likely to lose his patience with her neighbor at any second. Not that she blamed him. "Barney, this is Linc Rider. He's going to be working for me for a while ... as a handyman."

For a moment Barney's eyes just bulged in obvious surprise. "Well, I ain't working right now. You could've hired me." Then he squinted his eyes half-closed and grinned at her in a liquored-up fashion. "I could've fixed you up real good, honey bun. I know just what a widow like you needs." He reached for Jillian, but she sidestepped his action. "And you wouldn't even have to pay me, if you didn't want to. I'd be happy to oblige."

Suddenly Linc Rider was standing between her and Barney. The pleased, drunken expression on Barney's face quickly evaporated into complete surprise as the man found himself being jerked off the floor by the front of his black-and-red plaid shirt. Linc Rider glared into his startled expression. "That's enough. Now apologize to the lady," Linc said through clenched teeth. "And make it fast."

For several long seconds the two men stared at each other and it was during that time that Jillian realized all hell was about to break loose right there in the middle of the store. She couldn't allow that to happen. She had Gram and Eric to think about. "Please don't," she said, placing her hand on Linc Rider's arm.

But still he didn't loosen his hold on her neighbor. Instead he ground out, "Apologize to her."

Finally Barney mumbled, "I—I'm sorry, Jillian."

Linc jerked harder on the front of Barney's shirt. "Tell her it won't happen again."

"I-it won't happen again," Barney said, sounding like an old parrot who had come to hate having to mimic its owner.

Without removing his volatile glare from Barney, Linc released him and the man stumbled back, his face becoming enraged as he regained his balance. He straightened the front of his shirt and glowered at Linc. Then his glare shifted to Jillian. "You should have told me you were in need of a man. I'da been more than glad to help you out."

"Why, you bastard!" Linc said, starting forward. But this time, Jillian caught his arm and held on.

"Let him go. Please. He's been drinking. My mother-in-law will become upset if there's a commotion."

Linc's expression was hard with anger. "Then get out of here," he growled at Barney. "And make damn sure you're sober the next time you come inside."

Barney picked up his cap that had fallen on the counter during the struggle. Then, cursing under his breath, he stormed out. A few seconds later his motorcycle roared to life.

Jillian drew in a deep, steadying breath. Damn that Barney Langford. Something was going to have to be done about him. He couldn't continue to come into her store like that any time he pleased. For heaven's sake, he was going to have the whole town talking about them. As it was, she was embarrassed to face Linc Rider.

She owed the man her thanks. He had defended her when he could have just as easily walked away. And now that she gave it any thought at all, Jillian wondered if she could have handled Barney in his drunken state without the man's help.

But of course she could have, she told herself a second later. She'd done it plenty of times before. So what if Barney had seemed to be more intoxicated than usual? "Thank you for helping," she said self-consciously. "I can't imagine what's gotten into Barney. We're...we're just neighbors. That's all."

Linc was still staring in the direction Barney had disappeared, but now he turned those blue eyes of his in her direction. "I got a pretty good idea what's gotten into him. And I can tell you one thing—you're not rid of him yet. He's going to give you plenty of trouble until he gets what he wants."

Jillian shook her head. "Barney's just Barney. I've known him all my life. He's a lot of things, but I've never known him to be crazy about any woman for longer than a day or two. By tomorrow, he'll have forgotten all about this."

"I'm not so sure about that," Linc said, his blue eyes still hinting at the anger he'd felt toward the man only moments ago. "A woman can get into a man's blood. If that happens, he's liable to do just about anything to have her. I've seen it happen before."

"Really?" Jillian said, suddenly feeling breathless at the thought of a man desiring her that much. No man had ever had her in his blood. What would it be like to have a man that hot for you? If Barney was the answer to that question, then she could do without knowing, thank you, world, just the same. However, if Linc was—

"Well, when do I start?"

"Start? Uh, start what?"

"The job. When do you want me to begin, now or in the morning?"

"Oh, that," Jillian replied with a nervous laugh. Now, what was the old saying? *Out of the frying pan, into the fire.* "I just said that to get Barney out of here. I didn't think you'd take me seriously. I'm sorry if you did."

"I take everything seriously, Jillian."

His use of her name when she hadn't mentioned it to him startled her. But only for a moment. After all, Barney had been here just moments ago and though she couldn't recall right off, he had probably spouted her name at various times during their encounter. No doubt that was where Linc Rider had heard it.

He offered her his hand. "Look, what have you got to lose? Three meals a day is a bargain price and you know it."

"I just don't think this is such a good idea," Jillian found herself saying as she took his outstretched hand into hers. It was warm, but callused. The man was used to hard labor, there was no doubt about that. Maybe she could use his help, just for a day or two. Just to patch up a few leaks, mend a few broken windowpanes. *Just to fill this need inside her.* She did owe him her gratitude. "What kind of accommodations will you be needing?"

This time his grin was seductive. "Whatever you're willing to provide."

She straightened her shoulders. "It won't be much, Mr. Rider."

His gaze lingered on her face. "I'm sure it'll be more than enough."

Her complexion burned. Somehow his intense gaze seemed to lacerate her stomach from her other body parts and it floated slowly down to her knees. She wasn't playing with just plain, ordinary fire here. The man was like a laser. And, heaven help her, she was quick to recall that science had been her worst subject in school. Protons and atoms baffled her. Lasers terrified her. And in many ways she *was* terrified of this blue-eyed stranger who had just walked into her life. But in so many other ways, she found herself fascinated. There wasn't a man like him within a hundred miles of Pine Creek, and something—maybe the lonely woman deep inside her—wanted to keep him around for just a while longer.

"Look," she said, licking her dry lips. "There's a kitchen out back. It isn't very big. We use it about once or twice a month. That's when we make fresh sausage and boudin. I think there might be enough room in it for a sleeping bag. But there's no bathroom," she added quickly. "And no air conditioner."

"Sounds cozy. I'll make do," he drawled, and for the first time Jillian realized that his accent clearly stated that he was from somewhere in the Deep South, too.

"Whereabouts are you from?" she asked innocently.

"Biloxi, ma'am. Biloxi, Mississippi."

"Oh," Jillian replied.

What a coincidence, she thought to herself. She'd always felt a kind of kinship with Biloxi. Probably because she knew that Eric was born there, as were his biological parents. And though there hadn't been any communication between them, as far as she knew, Eric's birth mother still lived there. His natural father, she knew, had been killed in a car accident before he was born. "I've only been to Biloxi once in my life," she said.

"Oh? When was that?"

"About twelve years ago," she replied.

Jillian allowed herself to recall that happy time in her life, as she often did. Just as birth mothers had their stories of rushing to the hospital for the delivery of their child, she had her own wonderful memories of the hours it had taken her and Henry to make the anxious trip to Biloxi to get their son. She had planned Eric's future that day. "That's where my son was born. My husband and I went to pick him up when he was ten days old." She smiled at the memory. "You see, Eric's adopted."

"Is that right?" Linc said. And for the next few moments, there was only silence while his eyes drilled into hers. Then, lifting one corner of his mouth in a slight grin, he dropped his gaze slowly to her body. "You know something?'' he finally said, smiling at her. "I've got this strange feeling that you and I have something in common.''

His voice weaved a kind of magic around her. He smelled of wind and fresh air. Jillian's smile was open, friendly. "Do you, now?''

His grin widened. "I sure do.''

"And what might that something be?''

He stepped closer, all the while gazing into her eyes. "Need, Jillian. We both have a similar need.''

Her heart was pounding erratically. "Not me. I don't need a thing.''

"Really?'' he asked, his all-knowing gaze searching her face. "And what about your overly friendly neighbor? Don't you need someone to protect you from him?''

"I can handle Barney Langford,'' she said breathlessly. And in that moment she knew that the next time her pesky neighbor came into her store, drunk or not, she would handle him just fine.

The real problem was, could she handle a guy who had earned himself the nickname of Easy Rider?

Or more to the point, did she dare even try?

Chapter Three

Linc hurried outside. He had told his new employer that he wanted to guide his Harley to the back of the store and park it alongside the outdoor kitchen he would be using. She had followed him to the front entrance and directed him around the right side of the building.

But the truth was, he had needed fresh air, as dry and as dusty as it was, and he took several deep gulps of it, filling his lungs to capacity and hoping that the life-giving gas stabilized the emotional turmoil inside him. Seeing his kid for the first time had...well...had humbled him as nothing ever had.

The boy had made honor roll.

If that didn't beat all.

And all-star, too.

Linc could hardly believe it. *His kid*. His own flesh and blood. Wouldn't his mother have been both surprised and pleased to know about Eric?

Eric. It was a good, strong name. He liked it. Jillian Fontenot had done well to give it to his son.

His kid looked like him. Maybe his adoptive mother didn't see the resemblance; maybe she simply didn't want to, which at the moment was just fine for everyone concerned. She'd have to accept the truth soon enough.

Actually, he and Eric were a lot alike. Even in school, Linc knew he hadn't been a dummy. Not really. At least, not in the beginning when he was still in grade school and he had convinced himself that if he studied hard enough, he could grow up to be somebody.

But eventually, around the age of thirteen, around the time that his mother started getting sick, the streetwise kid inside him won out and the boy who had wanted to make something of himself had vanished behind the tough exterior he began to present to the world. But at least, he reminded himself, he'd kept his promise to his mother and had managed to graduate from high school.

Still, for the most part, growing up hadn't been easy. The main rule of the street gang in his neighborhood had been survival of the fittest. And, as far as he knew, it still was. But when a kid comes from a part of town where even the school officials use the word smart only as the first of two words to describe a student with a sharp tongue, a kid begins to think that studying is just a waste of time. Those few students who had dared come to class scrubbed clean and wearing decent clothes like his son probably did each day had been made fun of by the hoods Linc had hung around with.

But his kid would grow up to be somebody. He'd sure see to that.

But not if you take him away from all he knows, Linc's conscious whispered.

That same nagging voice had been bugging him for weeks now. Get lost! he argued back.

Don't you see? the voice continued. *If you take Eric away from here, he'll become just like you. A drifter. A nobody.*

No, Linc thought, continuing to fight. I'm his father. I won't let that happen. I'll be with him every step of the way. I'll teach him the ropes.

With what? the voice retorted. *With your street-smart diploma that has a major in skid row? Oh, sure, that ought to get the kid high on the corporate ladder to success.*

Shut up! Linc thought. Just shut up.

He had to get his act together. After all these years, he wasn't about to allow some nagging voice inside him to be his guiding force. His son was his only concern. Not the woman who had given him a home. So it looked as though she'd been a good parent. Well, now it was his turn to do right by his son.

Guiding his motorcycle to the back of the building, he swerved around the corner and saw the outdoor kitchen he would be using. The white paint on the exterior was peeling and Linc felt certain that the building had probably seen its better days some twenty years ago. There was one window with a broken pane, and the entrance door hung on one hinge and had to be propped closed.

Surprisingly, though, when he entered he found that the interior was well scrubbed and organized. No peeling paint hanging from the walls and ceiling as he'd imagined. The concrete floor had a drain located at its center and the two large aluminum sinks against one wall were the same size as that he'd used when he had worked for a while as a dishwasher in a restaurant in New Orleans. That had been years ago. Actually, the same summer that he joined the army. Several large pots and heavy-duty, long-handled utensils hung from hooks on the wall near the huge gas stove. Everything, absolutely everything in the room looked sanitized.

He'd slept in worse places.

Dropping his duffel bag to the floor, he rolled out the old army blanket that he'd brought along. It would serve as his bed during his stay, though it wasn't nearly thick enough to soften the floor beneath it. But, as he'd said to Eric's mother—funny, how he now thought of Jillian and not Trixie as being his son's mother—he'd make do. But first things first. Jillian Fontenot had offered him supper just before he'd walked out to get his things and he'd eagerly accepted. In his hurry to arrive in Pine Creek, he'd skipped lunch and as a result was now starving. To him, hot dogs and chili sounded like a gourmet meal. But the best part about his being at the supper table this evening was that he would be near his son. He was starving for that even more.

He found a plastic container inside one of the aluminum sinks, filled it with water and began soaping his hands and forearms. He rinsed away the suds, splashed several handfuls of cool water over his face, combed his hair back with his fingers and then rubbed the back of his neck with the palm of his hand. After the long ride through Louisiana's heat, the cool water felt refreshing.

He snatched a white towel hanging on a nearby nail and dried himself. He really would have preferred a hot, muscle-soothing shower, but he'd have to do without one for tonight. The detective he'd hired to help locate Eric had mentioned the camping facilities at a nearby state park. Tomorrow he'd go there and check them out. But if there weren't any showers, then he'd have to make do for the next few days with a swim in one of the nearby bayous.

Suddenly he found himself wondering if Jillian Fontenot had ever gone skinny-dipping in any of those bayous.

Probably not. Her spring was undoubtedly wound too tight. She would never allow herself to have that much fun.

She wasn't his type. The woman probably didn't even own a garter belt, much less a black one. Too bad. And the grandma-style bra he'd seen through the thin fabric of her blouse certainly wasn't French-cut. Pity. Her prim-and-proper upbringing probably prevented her from having the slightest idea of the countless ways a woman could entice a man by wearing such feminine attire.

To the woman's credit, though, she was slim and firm— and while he hadn't thought about it before now, he realized he liked that about her. Actually, he liked it a lot.

Linc had always felt he could read women well. After all, he had been around them all his life. And this woman was like an open book. In fact, he was willing to bet just about anything that she didn't have the slightest notion that her wide brown eyes smoldered with a fiery passion.

Suddenly realizing the direction his thoughts had taken, he quickly stopped all tender thoughts of her. Jillian Fontenot was simply a barrier he had to overcome to have his son. In a way, he was sorry about that—about having to deceive her—but life had taught him one thing. No one was going to take care of Linc Rider if *he* didn't. So what if he'd felt a strange, sudden warmth when he'd thought of her eyes and the passion they held in their depths. The whole darned circumstances for his being here were strange.

He dried the plastic pail he'd used, then the aluminum sink. Assured he was leaving everything just as he'd found it, he headed toward the house.

Eric answered his knock and Linc's heart pounded wildly at the sight of him. He stepped inside and Eric immediately led him to a thin, older woman with gray hair who was sitting in a wooden rocker. Before being introduced to her, Linc quickly glanced to the right and saw Jillian standing at the stove, stirring a spoon in a speckled black-and-white enamel pot that was set on one of the gas burners.

"Linc, this is my grandmother. But everyone calls her Gram. You can, too," Eric said. "Huh, Gram?"

The aging woman took her good time in scrutinizing Linc, starting from the top of his dark head and continuing down until she reached his feet.

"It's a pleasure to meet you, ma'am," Linc said, rocking back on the heels of his worn biker boots, hating the idea that he was being judged so quickly and so thoroughly by someone he didn't even know. He could see the measuring look in her eyes, and it made him uneasy, put him on the defensive. Dammit, nothing ever changed. These people were no different from all the other holier-than-thou folks he'd come in contact with over the years. It was a good thing he had come to the rescue of his son before these narrow-minded people warped Eric's way of thinking.

"Young man, my daughter-in-law tells me you're willin' to work for food. Is that right?"

"Yes, ma'am. Three meals a day."

The old woman nodded. "Well, I think that's more than fair. Why, in my day, we worked for a lot less."

"But that was sixty years ago, Gram," Jillian said over her shoulder. "Times have changed."

"Well, that's what's wrong with this country today. Everyone wants somethin' for nothin'. Hard work. That's what this country needs. Plenty of good old-fashioned hard work."

"Yes, Gram," Jillian replied as she tossed a speculative glance at Linc. He gave her an understanding nod.

Linc noticed the blouse Jillian was wearing was different from the one she'd worn earlier. Apparently she'd taken the time to wash up for supper, too. This blouse was navy with white polka dots. She'd combed her hair into a ponytail and tied it with a white, fringed scarf that made her look years younger than the age he knew she was. Still, he preferred the shiny brown mass hanging down to her shoulders as it had earlier. It was sexier looking.

"I'm sorry your first meal isn't something more hearty," Jillian said, placing a small platter of hot wieners on the table.

Her voice jarred Linc back to the present, and he was grateful for the distraction. He glanced at his son, then down at the floor.

Jillian set a bowl of steaming chili right next to the platter of smoking franks. As the spicy aroma filled his nostrils, Linc's stomach growled with hunger. "It sure smells good," he said. "I hope you didn't go through any extra trouble because of me."

"I didn't," she replied. "But there's plenty, so help yourself."

"We always have leftovers," Eric chimed in.

"Oh, yeah?" Linc replied, using any opportunity he found to gaze over in the boy's direction. He loved the sound of Eric's voice. He found himself almost mesmerized by it. But he had to be careful. The last thing he wanted to do was make anyone suspicious of the attention he gave the boy.

As it was, he already had Eric's face memorized and knew that tonight when he closed his eyes to sleep, the boy's features would be clear in his mind, down to the finest detail. His son had his blue eyes, the same ones Linc's mother had said he had gotten from the father he had never known. Linc knew he would be able to recall in detail the mole on his son's left cheek, the faint scar just under his chin that was less than half an inch long. He wondered what accident had put that scar there? Had Eric needed stitches? If so, had he cried when he got them? Or had he held his pain and fear inside him like Linc knew he would have done at that age? Had Jillian been there for him?

He knew the answer to the last question. One thing Linc felt he already knew about Jillian Fontenot—she loved her son—his son. Undoubtedly, she had been there for him.

Linc stopped himself, cursing inwardly. He hated it when his thoughts of Jillian softened. He hated having to admit that she looked to be a loving, giving person, because that meant if he continued with his plan, he was going to crush her. Distance, he told himself sharply. He had to keep his thoughts of her abstract. He had to think of her as an object in his way. It was easier to carry out his plan that way.

What a low-down bastard you are, his inner voice piped in.

Linc ground his teeth together and immediately forced that thought to the back of his mind. He *could not* let the woman be his concern.

"Let's eat," Jillian said, helping her mother-in-law to the table. Linc stood until she sat across from him and then he took a seat. Eric dropped into a chair next to him and their arms grazed as he did so.

"Sorry," Eric said politely, glancing up to meet Linc's gaze.

"No problem," Linc replied, immediately grabbing control of the emotional jolt that the casual contact had produced within him. Even so, his hand trembled slightly as he picked up his fork. His first instinct had been to encircle Eric's shoulders and pull his son against him in a show of affection. Dammit, but he felt like jumping up and punching a hole in the wall with his fist from having to stop himself from hugging his own son. Instead, he just grinned at Eric and the boy smiled back as he reached for a hot-dog bun.

"Eric," his mother said in a voice that spoke with the authority only a parent could have. "First, we say grace."

"Oh, yeah," Eric replied sheepishly, yanking back his hand and dropping his head in reverence. "I almost forgot."

Linc released his fork. *Grace before meals?* She was kidding, right? But just as his son had done, he dropped his head to his chest at the same time that his hands came to rest in his lap.

The one and only other time in Linc's life that he remembered praying had been when his mother had died. In his grief he had gone to a nearby church and had prayed for her soul. He'd known that she'd done a lot of things in this world that, according to polite society, she shouldn't have. Linc had understood that. He'd understood her. And if, indeed, there was a God in the heavens above, Linc sure hoped He did, too.

Suddenly Linc realized that Jillian was reciting a brief prayer. At the end of it both Gram and Eric joined in by saying, "Amen." Linc quickly cleared his throat and repeated the same word a half a second behind them.

"Help yourself, Mr. Rider," Jillian said. "We're not very formal at mealtime—nor at any other time, as far as that goes."

For Linc, that was sure good to hear. Formal was about as far from his way of life as Pluto was from the sun. Still, this family's quiet manners—and their prayers—were making him feel downright uncomfortable.

"Then could we start being less formal by having everyone here at the table call me Linc?"

"Does that end with a *c* or a *k?*" Eric asked, an inquisitive expression on his face. A moment later he took a big bite of his hot dog.

"A *c.*"

The boy chewed a couple more times and then swallowed his whole mouthful of food at once. "My name ends with a *c,* too. That's neat. Huh, Mom?"

Without looking at her son, Jillian poured chili over her wiener. "I guess so, Eric."

"Well, I think it's kind of neat. Don't you, Linc?"

"Sure, kid."

Something about this scene bothered Jillian. What did she really know about this man, this stranger she had allowed into their home? Nothing. Absolutely nothing. Well, as his employer, she had a right to know certain things. She poured Gram a glass of milk. "Do you have a regular job, Mr. Rider?" she asked.

Linc shook his head. "You mean, when I'm not looking up old friends?" He grinned. "Yeah, I have a regular job. And not only does it pay well, but the benefits are good, too."

The way he was smiling at her made Jillian feel as though she were being a nosy so-and-so, which simply wasn't true.

It was just that "easy" attitude of his. It reminded her a lot of Barney Langford, which wasn't exactly something she cared to sing about. Yet, even as she thought it, she knew there wasn't any way that Linc Rider and Barney Langford could have been categorized together. Barney was ordinary, and pesky, to boot. But Linc Rider was in a league all his own. He was wild and dangerous, and, if the truth be told, he affected her in ways she didn't want to think about.

She shouldn't have hired him.

And she should just fire him now.

Right this minute.

Right here on the spot.

But she didn't make one move to do so. Somehow she knew she'd live to regret it.

After supper Eric went outside to water the vegetable garden that was grown each year to help supply the store with fresh tomatoes, bell peppers and cucumbers. When Gram's arthritis was as painful as it was today, Jillian always helped her to bed immediately after supper. Then she returned to the kitchen and found Linc clearing the dirty dishes from the kitchen table and placing them in the sink.

"I'll do that," she replied, hurrying to remove the soiled plates that he'd already stacked together. In her rush, she knocked over an empty glass that had been set on the edge of the table. It smashed to pieces on the worn linoleum floor. "Oh, darn," she said. "How clumsy of me." Embarrassed, she stooped over and began picking up the broken glass.

"Let me help," Linc said, placing the remainder of the dishes in the sink. He squatted down next to her. "Hey, you'd better be careful that you don't cut yourself."

Oh, for heaven's sake, Jillian thought. Was the man dense, or what? Didn't he know it was his presence that rattled her?

She had no sooner had that thought when she felt a prick at the end of one finger. "Ouch!" she exclaimed.

Linc Rider grabbed her injured hand. "See? You've cut yourself."

"It's nothing," Jillian replied, quickly using a clean napkin from the table to stop the bleeding. Still, tears rolled down her cheeks. Tears that were brought on from frustration and fatigue, and not from any kind of pain associated with her injury. She wiped at the moisture that gathered in her eyes with the back of her hand. "I'll get the broom and sweep up this mess," she said, rising to her full height.

Linc followed her lead, towering about three inches above her head. "Let me see," he said, reaching out once more for her wounded hand.

"Please don't," she whispered breathlessly, suddenly jerking her hand free of his and wiping it down the side of her skirt. Their gazes locked for a moment.

Then Jillian looked away. "Just don't touch me. Please."

Angered by her tone of voice, Linc stepped back. What was her problem? Did she think he was a damned disease or something? "Lady, I may look it to you, but I can assure you that I'm not contagious."

By now her complexion was the color of ripe tomatoes. "I—I'm sorry," she stammered. "I know you just wanted to help. But it's nothing. See...?" Now she offered him her hand, palm up, to examine. The smile on her face was forced.

And he knew it. Besides, his temper was smoldering and he was ready for a good fight, if that was what she wanted. "In other words, look the merchandise over, but don't touch?"

Jillian took a deep breath. She'd started this, but it was as good a time as any to set some ground rules. "Let me make one thing perfectly clear. If you want this job as much as you say, then make sure you understand me. I may be a widow, but I'm not fair game for you, or any man. Keep your hands on the job—period. Do I make myself clear?"

"Perfectly, ma'am," Linc retorted, his angry glare slicing down the length of her. At that moment it would have been the thrill of his life to bring her down a notch or two. It would serve her right if he loosened that tightly wound spring of hers.

Linc continued to glare at her, though not quite sure just yet who he was the most angry with. Her, for not wanting to be touched, or himself, for wanting to touch her so badly.

But he didn't dare seek the answer. Instead he turned, sauntered toward the back door and walked outside without a backward glance, allowing the door to slam shut behind him.

Shaken more than she wanted to admit, Jillian finished cleaning the kitchen. She shouldn't have hired the man at any price, she told herself. He was going to be trouble, pure and simple. Even Gram thought so. But then, Gram was always worried that a stranger was going to be trouble.

Jillian inhaled deeply. She'd just have to keep her guard up—and her eyes open.

Walking outside, she was surprised to find Eric talking with Linc. When he spotted her, he dropped the water hose he held and ran toward her, excitement shining brightly in his eyes.

"Linc said he's gonna ride me on his motorcycle, Mom. Boy, wait till I tell Wally."

Halting in her tracks, Jillian frowned. "No way, Eric." Then she turned her glare toward Linc. How dare he offer to take her son on some wild motorcycle ride without asking her permission first? Just who did he think he was?

"Now, Eric," Linc said, tucking his hands into the back pockets of his jeans. "You're jumping the gun. I said you'd have to ask your mama first, remember?"

"Can I, Mom?"

"No," Jillian repeated sternly. "Absolutely not."

"Oh, please, Mom."

"The answer is no, Eric." Jillian turned furious eyes in Linc's direction. "Next time you get some wild idea that concerns my son, I'd appreciate it if you'd check it out with me before you go filling his head with all sorts of ideas."

"He didn't mean nothing by it, Mom," Eric said, his voice pleading with her not to be upset with his new friend.

Linc gazed at her. "Look, he's right. I didn't mean anything by it," he said sincerely. "We were just talking. I should have checked with you first. Next time—"

"There won't *be* a next time. Eric's days are as filled as mine. He doesn't have time for any other activities. And besides, I didn't hire you to entertain my son. He's not to bother you, and I hope you will give him the same courtesy." She faced Eric. "Now finish up and get inside. It's getting late."

Eric hung his head. "Yes, ma'am." He rolled up the hose and hung it on a nearby hook. Then he headed for the house. When the door closed behind him, Jillian turned back to Linc, determination lining her face. "My son is at an impressionable age. You come riding in here on a motorcycle without a care in the world and try to undermine my authority over him. To a boy Eric's age, your way of life seems exciting. But not to me."

"That's rather obvious."

Jillian sighed. She was handling this all wrong. "Eric's a good boy. I won't have his head filled with foolishness. Just stay away from him."

"Is that a threat?"

Jillian's heart began pounding. Perhaps she *had* made a mistake in hiring Linc. "I think you'd better get on that motorcycle right now and ride out of here."

"Well, you see . . . I'd do that, ma'am, if I thought it was the right thing. But to be perfectly honest, you need my help—and I need yours."

"You can't stay here if I say you have to go."

"Would you do that just to please yourself? Even if it ends up being at your son's expense?"

Guilt swelled up inside her. "What do you mean by that?"

"It's obvious that someone's going to have to help you get some repairs done around here. Aren't you planning to keep your word to Eric about his being able to play baseball?"

"Well, of course—"

"Then the answer seems simple to me."

Jillian stiffened. She knew he was right. "If I decide to let you stay, do you think you can remember the rules?"

He took a step toward her, a strange light in his eyes. "Let's see. You're off-limits, Eric's off-limits. How about the old lady? I guess she's off-limits, too, huh?"

Jillian wasn't about to play this kind of game with him. She whirled around to go, but instead she felt fingers of steel close around her wrist, found herself being jerked back against a hard, male body. Her eyes shot to his face.

"Hey, loosen up! You're looking at me like I'm some-body else's dirty laundry. Is that your way of trying to deny the fact that you just might be liking what you see?"

Jillian's whole body went weak. "Of course not. And you have some nerve—"

"So I've been told."

"Why, you—"

Jillian jerked herself free from his hold. She was on fire—burning up. She could barely think straight, such was his effect on her. Belatedly she realized that was why she was so on the defensive. Linc was making her feel things she'd never felt before. And despite her daydreaming about his hunky looks, she knew only trouble lay in those mesmerizing blue eyes for a simple girl like her. Backing away quietly, she decided retreat was the better part of valor right now.

"Hey, are you all right?" she heard him yell at her just as she reached the back door of the house.

Huh. Hell would freeze over before she'd give him the benefit of an answer.

Chapter Four

For Jillian, the night was hot and miserable in spite of the air-conditioning unit down the hall that hummed a dull, steady tune in its attempt to cool off the house to a decent temperature now that total darkness had finally claimed victory for a few short hours. As a result, the bodice of the thin, white cotton slip she always slept in was damp with perspiration.

Unconsciously Jillian tugged at the cotton lace that crisscrossed over her breasts and disappeared into the side seams just under the hollows of her arms. Her skin burned against the delicate white fabric. She wished to God she could find some kind of relief from the humid heat. Relaxing would probably have helped some, but she was too keyed up to do that.

Which brought her to the next problem. Since coming to bed she hadn't been able to close her eyes on one occasion without thinking about Linc. At times, even thinking about him in ways that would have been embarrassing, if anyone had known. She wished she could just close her eyes and go to sleep. Unfortunately, tonight that one simple luxury seemed to elude her completely.

What in the world had she done to deserve such torment? Were a few frivolous thoughts of *what if her life had been different* worth such punishment? She sure didn't think so.

Well, she'd show Mr. *Easy* Rider a thing or two. She wasn't as naive and helpless as he seemed to think she was. Maybe she wasn't well traveled. And maybe she hadn't known great passion in her lifetime. Maybe she wasn't even meant to, but did that make her any less of a woman? Definitely not.

Jillian folded her arms under her breasts in an attempt to cradle herself. She felt like crying and didn't really know why. Maybe because some little voice inside her was saying it was time she faced reality. That Henry had been right all along when he'd said she was a hardy woman. Plain and simple. With no frills attached.

Now near tears, Jillian turned on her other side. It wasn't that she minded being called hardy. Hardy was good. It just...well, alone it didn't sound...very feminine. It certainly didn't come close to describing the way she felt inside.

Growing frustrated with herself, she rolled over again and this time her cotton slip twisted under her and she had to lift her hips from the white muslin sheet beneath her to straighten her clothing. Now lying flat on her back, she lifted her hands close to her face to examine them in the dark. They felt dry and neglected and were undoubtedly a far cry from the kinds of hands a man would admire. Especially a man like Linc Rider. He probably liked his women all soft and cuddly. A *hardy* woman like herself didn't stand a chance.

Which certainly was fine with her, Jillian told herself while reaching for a bottle of thick, creamy lotion on the small round table next to her bed. She'd gotten the bottle from the cosmetics shelf in the store and had placed it there more than a month ago, promising herself that, before retiring each night, she'd make use of it. Faithfully. Well, so much for good intentions. The bottle was still full. And her hands were still chafed. Frowning at her lack of determination—or maybe it was simply lack of interest on her part—she replaced the bottle on the nightstand. Applying lotion on her hands once in a blue moon wasn't going to do them any good.

Anyway, who was she trying to kid? Tomorrow she'd be washing dishes ... mopping floors ... cleaning bathrooms. All the lotion in the world wasn't going to soften her hands—or her life.

Turning to see the small alarm clock next to her bed, she saw it was past midnight. Sighing, she turned back in the other direction.

This was all *his* fault, showing up like he had, insisting that she hire him and making her feel tickled pink to be a woman. He was a total stranger, for heaven's sake. A rebel. Firing him first thing in the morning was the only sensible thing she could do. The trouble was, she hadn't felt sensible from the moment he'd walked into her store. But surely, if she did fire him, then once he was on his way, she would feel like her old self again. And, in no time at all, she wouldn't even remember his name.

At least, she hoped the latter was true. But then again, she had her doubts. Because now the man in those strange, erotic dreams that she'd been having lately would have a face. And a name. Easy.

For Linc, the night was long and hot, in spite of the fact that he'd propped the kitchen door open and placed his blanket where the small breeze that periodically blew outside would venture in and give him some relief. He was down to his jockey shorts. Even that didn't help. He was tempted to move his blanket outdoors.

He had to stop thinking of her—period.

His son was his first and only reason for being in this hot, dusty little nothing town. So why was Jillian sneaking into his thoughts, too, when he least expected it? It was obvious the woman was scared to death of him. He'd seen that petrified what-if-he-touches-me look that had come over her face when he'd made a step in her direction.

But, heaven help him, he'd wanted to touch her. Actually, at the precise moment when he'd caught her by the arm, he'd wanted it so badly, he'd almost felt possessed. Possessed by a woman he'd once called a country bumpkin. That almost made him angry with himself. And with her.

She was in his blood.

No way, he argued back.

Agitated, Linc rose, jerked up his blanket from the hard concrete floor and carried it outdoors. He didn't care if he was wearing only his jockey shorts. He'd be darned if he'd just sit there and allow such ridiculous thoughts to dominate his thinking.

It was a typical Southern night, hot and still, with only a small breeze blowing every now and then. The sound of locusts filled the silence. From a distance an owl hooted, and a large armadillo scurried across the ground only a few feet in front of Linc and disappeared into the darkness.

Stretching his arms to the sky to ease the stiffness in his muscles, Linc groaned. Then he began settling his blanket over the top of a sturdy-looking redwood picnic table located near the vegetable garden his son had watered earlier. He was still making himself as comfortable as possible on his new makeshift bed when he heard the sound of a door opening.

He glanced toward the house, waiting to see who was coming out the back door. When he recognized Eric, relief swept through him. He watched the boy in silence until he was certain that Eric had come in search of him before saying, "Pssst...Eric. I'm over here." His voice was low, so as not to awaken anyone in the house. Having another confrontation with Jillian so soon wasn't exactly what he had in mind for a late-night snack.

Eric froze at the sound of Linc's voice, looked around the backyard until he spotted him, and then hurried over, clutching a pillow to his chest. "I thought you were sleeping in the outdoor kitchen," he whispered.

Linc shook his head. "Too hot in there."

Eric held out the pillow to him. "I thought you could use this. I was gonna bring it out as soon as my mom went to bed, but I fell asleep first. Sorry."

Linc took the pillow from him. "Thanks, kid. It'll come in handy for the rest of the night."

"I hope so," Eric said, his grin matching that of the man beside him. "Are you going to be staying with us a long time?"

"Probably not."

"Oh," Eric said disappointedly, dropping his head down until his chin almost rested on his chest. "I was hoping...I mean...I thought maybe..." He looked up at Linc. "Is it because my mom said you couldn't?"

"Your mama's hired me to do a few needed repairs. After that, I'll be on my way," Linc said, calming his pounding heart and wishing he could tell his son the truth. Soon— very soon—the two of them would be leaving together.

Hadn't he known his son would respond to him like this?

"Okay, but if it's my mom that you're worried about, she's not nearly as bad as she sounds. Gram says she's just got a lot on her mind these days."

"Yeah?" replied Linc, noting the forgiving tone in Eric's voice. His hopes sank. His son's concern wasn't for him. It was for his mother. The kid cared a lot about her. Linc's gut knotted up. "Your mama isn't the problem, Eric."

Eric didn't say anything for a few moments, and Linc could tell that something was on his mind. Then, suddenly, as though someone had jerked the words from him, Eric blurted out, "Do you have any kids?"

Linc felt the wind rush from his lungs. Now what had prompted the boy to ask that question? "No kids. I'm not even married. Why?"

Eric shrugged. "Just asking, I guess."

"Sounds to me like you've got something on your mind," Linc said, gently probing.

Eric hesitated. "Well, yeah . . . kind of."

"Well, stop hee-hawing around. What gives?"

"It's kind of . . . well . . . it's kind of something that's man-to-man, if you know what I mean."

"Man-to-man?" Linc repeated, wondering what could possibly be on his son's mind at this late hour. He knew one thing, though. Whatever it was, it was the real reason the boy had sought him out in the first place. The pillow had been a mere ploy.

"Yeah," Eric said, swallowing hard. "It's about . . . well, you know . . ." Linc waited for him to continue. "It's about sex."

"Sex," Linc repeated, dumbfounded. Jeez, but he hadn't been prepared for that one. Not yet. Not tonight. Talk about being slapped in the face with a cold turkey. "Uh, look, Eric, I've been out of touch with boys your age for a long time. I think your mama would be better prepared to answer your questions on that subject."

"Not Mom. She's too busy in the store. Besides, she probably doesn't even know the answer."

"Yeah, well, I've got a bit of a surprise for you, kid. Believe me, parents know the answers."

Eric frowned. "Ah, I know that. It's just that...well..."

"Well, what?" Linc asked gruffly, his insides suffering from an emotional thunderstorm that was threatening to drown him. He took two deep breaths and waited.

Eric deepened his frown. "It's just that this is something just guys would know about. If my father were alive, I'd ask him. But not my mom. Not about this. It's too embarrassing."

Linc's chest felt heavy and for a moment he feared he might just smother to death right then and there. The kid had no idea what he was doing to him. Still, he shook his head in agreement. "Okay, maybe you have a point." Then, hoping to maintain complete control of his emotions, he said, "Look, Eric, maybe some other time we could talk about this. But right now—"

"I know," Eric cut in. "You're tired and want to go back to sleep. Grown-ups are always tired when a kid wants to talk about sex. Nobody ever wants to give us straight answers. I thought you'd be different. You seemed different from anyone I've ever known. But I was wrong." He turned to go.

Linc hesitated only a second before saying, "Hold it, kid." Then, coughing into his fist, he rubbed his eyes clear of what little sleep he'd had thus far. He peered at his wristwatch. "Okay, you win. Just what exactly do you want to know about sex at one-thirty in the morning?"

Eric hesitated and Linc instinctively knew he'd lost some of the boy's initial trust in him. In was understandable. He'd have felt the same way if the shoe had been on the other foot.

Finally, Eric looked up at him and, after taking a deep breath, appeared to make a decision. "Do all guys really gotta do it by a certain age?"

Linc wasn't up-to-date on how the present generation of eleven-year-old boys thought, but he sure knew what this one meant without asking any further questions. "No, kid. Who told you that?"

"Jimmy Krandon's brother. He's sixteen, and when we all went camping a few weeks ago, he told me and Jimmy and Wally that we had to. Even if we didn't want to. He said it was the code of the West and we'd be called sissies if we didn't."

"Come here, kid, and sit down," Linc said, patting the hard table next to him. He shoved his hair back from his forehead and sighed. Eric did as he bade and Linc automatically placed an arm around the boy's shoulders. It felt good—natural—and right. Father and son. He and Eric. It *was* right. He felt it in his gut. "First off, there is no such code," Linc said quietly. "Jimmy Krandon's brother doesn't know what he's saying. He's just trying to act big in front of you all."

"Really?"

"Really."

Eric gave a relieved sigh. "I told Wally it wasn't true. But I wasn't really sure and Wally wouldn't ask his dad. We weren't scared, or nothing," he added quickly. "We were just wondering."

Linc's expression softened. He wanted to grin, but he kept his expression serious. "Yeah, I know how that can be. Now don't forget to tell Wally so he can stop worrying, too."

Eric rose to his feet. "Oh, I won't. And thanks, Linc. See you tomorrow." Then he ran toward the house and within a few seconds had slipped through the doorway.

"Anytime, kid," Linc replied, staring after him. "Anytime at all."

Linc eased back down on the tabletop and stared up at the star-studded sky, his hands folded and placed under the pillow that Eric had left for him. Kids and their curiosity about sex. It never changed. He remembered those days. Only the answers to his questions had come from the older punks on the streets who'd thought they'd had all the answers. But his son deserved better answers than that.

And he probably got them, his inner voice whispered back. *From his mother—Jillian. So just face the fact that your boy is better off right where he is.*

No, Linc thought, fighting back. He and his son belonged together. Already Eric was coming to him for advice and they hardly even knew each other. Wasn't that proof that the boy needed him?

Satisfied with his own argument, Linc closed his eyes and eventually dozed off, unaware that images of Eric—and sometimes of Jillian—played gently on his mind.

The trouble was that, even as he slept, he knew he had two choices. Unknowingly, he tossed and turned upon the hardwood table for the remainder of the night, trying to make a decision. Would he listen to his head? Or to his heart?

By morning, it was still a toss-up.

Breakfast consisted of hot coffee, pancakes, maple syrup and fried ham.

Linc sat at the kitchen table, wearing his same worn pair of jeans from yesterday. His navy T-shirt, however, was clean. In lieu of his biker boots, he had slipped into a pair of worn Nikes.

Jillian, dressed in another blue-jean skirt and a dark pink pullover sweater, hustled about the kitchen, flipping pancakes with one hand and turning the flame under a pot of grits with the other. On a back burner, ham slices sizzled in a black iron skillet.

Wanting to find a reason to dislike her, Linc sat at the kitchen table, watching her movements. Disliking her definitely would make life easier for him. Finally he decided that, indeed, he'd found something he didn't like about her. Her lips. They were too full. Too soft looking. Too inviting. He didn't want an invitation from her. He wanted his son.

Turning in his direction, her eyes met his, and his stomach turned over. Damn those eyes. And those inviting lips of hers. She walked over, served him a stack of pancakes and then returned to the stove.

"Eat up, Mr. Rider," she said over her shoulder. "It'll be a while before lunch."

Linc didn't hesitate. He poured warm maple syrup over his stack of pancakes from a small pint-size crock pitcher. He had never had warm syrup before in his life. Jillian returned to his side, holding the black iron skillet, and raked two thick slices of fried ham onto his plate.

As he ate, Linc continued watching Jillian as she went about her task of preparing breakfast. Obviously this wasn't her first time mixing a batch of pancakes, or dishing out a skillet of cured, browned pork. She moved about the kitchen with the earned self-confidence of a woman who knew her way around. He found himself admiring her skill and knew it came from years of caring for her family. With a start, he realized he was beginning to admire her skill as a housewife and a mother a whole lot more than he disliked her full, inviting lips. A whole lot more.

Eric joined him at the table and Jillian began filling his plate. "Drink all your milk," she said before turning to Linc and offering him a second helping. Which he accepted. And why not? He'd already admitted to himself that she was a good cook.

"It's been a long time since I've had to worry about feeding a man," she said, placing the platter of remaining pancakes at the center of the table. "I'd forgotten how much one can eat."

Swallowing, Linc looked up at her. "Sounds to me like you've been without a man around here for too long."

Jillian halted her movements. "Don't get any ideas, Mr. Rider." Then she removed the half-empty container of milk from the table and set it on the top shelf inside the refrigerator.

"Believe me, ma'am," Linc said as he rose from the table, "that would be hard for a man to do around here." As he walked outside, he let the screen door slam shut behind him. When he glanced back a few seconds later, he saw her watching him through the kitchen window over the sink. He knew she was still having second thoughts about hiring him. Somehow, he had to find a way to win her over before she changed her mind. But first, he needed to learn to keep his cool when around her.

Confident that he would, he began whistling a low tune as he went in search of the tools and materials he would need to do his job, in particular, a hammer and nails, a saw and a few scraps of wood. Not that his boss lady seemed in any hurry to give him direct orders as to what she wanted done. And not that he really needed her to.

"Can I help you, Linc?"

On hearing his son's voice, Linc whirled around. "Hey, kid."

"Well, can I?" Eric asked.

"Yeah, sure," Linc replied, playfully readjusting the baseball cap Eric wore on top of his head. He fought against the ever-present urge to pull the boy to him in an exuberant hug. "Do you know how to use a hammer?"

"Of course," Eric said indignantly. "My mom taught me."

"She teaches you everything, doesn't she?"

Eric shrugged. "I guess so. Even when my father was alive, he didn't spend much time with me. He was always working and all."

"But wasn't he the one who taught you how to play baseball?"

"Nope."

"Who did, then?"

"My mom."

Linc looked back at his son.

"She's pretty good for a girl," Eric assured him proudly.

Envy wasn't an emotion that Linc had expected to feel, and the fact that he did surprised him and made his voice sound gruff when he spoke. "So you think your mama's pretty terrific, huh?"

"Yeah, she's okay. Did she happen to tell you that I'm adopted?"

"She mentioned it," Linc said, keeping a tight rein on his emotions.

"I don't remember any of it. Of course, I was just a baby. But it's never been a secret and since I've gotten old enough to understand, Mom's told me everything she knows about it. My biological mother was from Biloxi, Mississippi. So was my biological father, but he was killed in a car wreck before I was born."

Linc felt as though he were smothering. "Is that so?"

"Yeah," Eric said, speaking in a matter-of-fact tone of voice.

Linc wondered how his brain could still be thinking straight when the rest of him felt so off kilter. The kid talked about his adoption as though it was no big deal. As though it was just an everyday part of his life. Not even at Eric's age had he been that nonchalant about not having a father, and he had the scars to prove it.

But just who in the hell made up that story about his having died in some car crash? Trixie? Or Jillian?

"Look, kid, I need to get to work. You'd better scram."

The surprise in Eric's gaze was evident. "But you said I could help," Eric replied, bending down to help gather up his share of the work materials that Linc had been placing together while they were talking.

"I know I said that. But now that I think about it, I'm not so sure that it's such a good idea. For one thing, your mama's not going to like it. Besides, don't you have other chores to do?"

"Well...yeah," Eric said, disappointment showing in the way he dropped his eyes to the ground. "Mom told me to walk over to Mrs. Bramley's and get the eggs she usually picks up each morning from her henhouse. Mrs. Bramley's sick today."

Linc felt like a pure heel for rejecting his son's offer to help. It damn sure wasn't what he wanted to do. And it was obvious the kid wanted to be around him, too. But then, Jillian had said to stay away from him, and it was too soon to risk getting her temper riled up again.

Still, Linc hated the idea of pushing his son away. He made a quick decision. "Hey, look, I'll hurry and do my chores, and you hurry and do yours. Then maybe later this afternoon, we can get together for some baseball. What do you say?"

Eric perked up with a grin. "Yeah. That's a good idea. Besides, I could use the practice. I'm not nearly as good as some of the other guys on my team."

"Oh, yeah? Well, we'll just have to see about changing that," Linc said, giving the boy a reassuring smile.

Eric continued grinning as he mumbled goodbye and ran off.

Gathering up a small sack of nails to go along with the hammer he needed, Linc walked around the side of the store. When he rounded the front corner, Jillian was standing at the entrance, looking out at the parking lot. "Why, Mr. Rider, I was wondering where you'd gone off to," she said, holding the door open for him to enter.

"The name's Linc," he said, waltzing through the opening she made for him in the doorway. He made sure he avoided touching her in any way. "I'd appreciate it if you'd call me that." He placed the hammer and nails on a shelf and gazed around the store. "So where should I start?" he said, feeling angry with himself for not having had the good sense to have known about Eric's birth from the start. And he was angry at Jillian, too, for looking so damned vulnerable. Man, he couldn't wait to slam a hammer against the heads of a few nails. Maybe it would ease this enormous pounding that was going on inside him. Damn her soft-looking mouth, not to mention her wide brown eyes. She looked almost frightened of him, as though she feared he was going to make her do something that she would later regret. "I don't bite, Jillian. I only growl."

It took a moment before his comment registered and she was able to manage a tentative smile. "No, I'm sure you don't bite."

That smile bothered him. A lot.

She looked away from him. "So, where do you think you should start first...Linc?" she said. "On the shelving?"

She'd called him by his first name. Now that was really a first. Things were definitely looking up. He'd begun to wonder if he'd ever break through that cool exterior of hers.

"Yeah, I think that's a good idea," he said, sauntering up to the first broken shelf he saw. He noticed Jillian following right behind him. And for some unknown reason he wasn't going to dwell on, her closeness bothered him almost as much as her smile had a minute ago. She smelled good. Sweet. Like warm maple syrup. He cleared his throat. "This one looks like it just needs a couple of nails."

"It broke yesterday morning and I was planning to fix it this weekend," Jillian replied. "I've been trying to keep up with the minor repairs." She sighed. "It's the big ones that have me concerned."

He lifted the end of the shelf that was sagging and held it in place. "You needn't be. I'll take care of them for you," Linc heard himself saying. He hammered in a long nail to secure the shelf, then he hammered in two more.

He wondered why she was standing at his back, practically breathing that soft, sweet-smelling breath of hers down his neck. Doing his best to ignore her, he set the last nail and gave it two light taps to secure it in place.

Jillian cleared her throat. "Are you sure you know what you're doing?"

So, she didn't think he had enough brains for the job, did she?

He glared back over his shoulder at her. "Yes, ma'am, I sure do."

Jillian seemed to get the message he wanted to convey without his having to say more. She took a step back. But when he turned to finish the job, he felt her move in closer.

Dammit! He didn't need an overseer.

Frustrated with her lack of faith in his ability as a carpenter, he whacked the hammer down on the nail head and, because his attention was elsewhere, right down on his finger, too.

"Oo-uch..." he bellowed, dropping the hammer and bringing his damaged finger automatically to his mouth for some quick soothing. The hammer landed on the end of one soft Nike, which, unfortunately for him, didn't provide enough cushion for the blow. "Ouch...dammit!" he cried out. Hobbling off on one foot, he shook his hand repeatedly to relieve the pain, using the other one to hold up his aching toes.

"For heaven's sake," Jillian sputtered, "are you all right?"

Linc sucked in a pain-filled breath through clenched teeth and didn't answer for several drawn-out seconds. "Yeah, I'm just dandy," he finally replied. "I like making myself miserable."

"Well, you don't have to be so testy about it," Jillian said, bracing her hands on her hips. "I was only trying to show some concern."

"Well, it's your fault to begin with. You didn't have to stand there, breathing down my neck."

Her mouth flew open. "I wasn't breathing down your neck."

"You were."

"I was not. How dare you insinuate such a thing!"

"Insinuate, hell. Lady, you *were* breathing down my neck. I damn sure know what a warm breath feels like."

"That's absolutely ridiculous. You're imagining things."

Before he could reply, she whirled around and headed for the checkout counter. But as quick as she obviously wanted to be, it wasn't quick enough. Linc had seen the tears that had sprung suddenly to her eyes. "Ah, the hell with it," he mumbled, bending over and picking up the hammer he had dropped, now more determined than ever to fix that broken shelf. If for no other reason than to show her that he could. Even without her supervision.

The morning wore on with Jillian and Linc speaking only when necessary. He was able to mend a total of five broken shelves. One shelf had split in two and was impossible to mend. He planned to make a new one.

Jillian stayed busy with the customers who came and went in a steady stream. Some only wanted a carton of milk, others a soft drink and still others a pack of cigarettes. Most didn't notice the handsome stranger who worked diligently, repairing the broken shelves throughout the store. But a couple of them noticed him right away and raised their eyebrows in surprise. Unfortunately for Jillian, having to answer their curious questions about her new handyman became an added chore she wasn't prepared for.

Around ten-thirty business had slowed down, so Jillian started lunch on the old gas range that was behind the counter. The stove had been there for as long as she could remember. Gram had used it for cooking when she was still a young bride and capable of working alongside her husband in the market. Today not only did Jillian still use it to prepare the family's meals when necessary, but she used it throughout the day to make coffee for herself and her customers in the same old drip porcelain pot that Gram had used for years. And it didn't matter the time of year. Even in midsummer, people in the area still liked their sips of coffee hot, thick and sweet, and as often as possible during the day.

Jillian had just added water to her pot of gravy steaks and replaced the lid when Wilma Jenkins walked in. The woman had on a pair of white skintight jeans and a snug orange tank top that she had tucked into her waistband. Her short,

bottle-dyed red hair and her carefully applied makeup made
her look worldly in comparison to most of the other women
in the area. Actually, Gram and some of her friends had
used a less complimentary word to describe the young, attractive divorcée, but at times, deep down inside, Jillian
wished she were more like her.

What woman wouldn't want to have men turn their heads
when she walked by? Simply put, Wilma Jenkins was sex
personified. Pine Creek's one-and-only claim to a sex kit-
ten. When there was a church social, none of the area wives
allowed their husbands to so much as talk to her. But did
Wilma let that stop her? Uh-uh. She just went right ahead
and spoke to all the husbands anyway. Or so Jillian had
heard. She hadn't ever attended any of the Saturday-night
church socials herself. Henry hadn't liked them, and after
his death, she simply hadn't wanted to go alone. Besides, she
was always too busy or too tired to care about such things.

"Hi, Jillian," Wilma said, stepping up to the counter.
"My usual brand, please."

"You want a pack or a carton?"

"Ahh...make it a carton this time. It'll save me from
having to stop in so often just for cigarettes."

Jillian nodded and then bent under the counter to get the
carton of Wilma's favorite brand of filtered cigarettes. While
she was still stooped over, she heard Wilma suck in a deep
breath.

"Who's the hunk?" Wilma asked as Jillian came up with
a red-and-white carton in her hand. But Wilma didn't even
bother to look in her direction.

Jillian's stomach sank to her knees. Never once in the two
years since Wilma had moved back to Pink Creek had Jillian felt any malice toward the woman like so many of the
other area women. But at that moment, if she could have
pulled out every strand of the woman's hair, rubbed her face

with mud and added twenty-five pounds of cellulite to her thighs, Jillian knew she would have done it. Linc Rider was *her* handyman. Wilma Jenkins had no right to have that gleam in her eyes when she looked at him. No right whatsoever.

"Here are your cigarettes," Jillian replied, ignoring her customer's question.

"Jillian, who *is* he?" Wilma insisted, now tiptoeing to get a better look at Linc over the two shelves of groceries separating them. "He's gorgeous."

"He's working for me—temporarily," Jillian replied calmly. But she felt anything but calm. "He'll only be around for a couple of days."

"Too bad," Wilma replied, glancing over at Jillian. "Is he taken?"

Jillian knew her face had to be turning the color of asparagus. She felt that possessive...that jealous of what Wilma was thinking. Which was totally ridiculous. "What do you mean?"

"Oh, come on, Jillian," Wilma replied breathlessly. "Does he have a wife or girlfriend?"

"No—I mean, I d-don't know," Jillian replied, feeling like a fool. She was stammering, for heaven's sake. But for some reason she had just assumed he wasn't involved or attached to anyone.

Well, actually, it was more than an assumption. Somehow she had known from the start that Linc Easy Rider wasn't committed to any woman. But to her way of thinking, it wasn't any of Wilma's business, one way or the other.

Well, if Ms. Wilma Jenkins was looking to find herself a man, she could just look elsewhere. Jillian would gladly mention her name to Barney Langford the next time he came into the store. The two of them would make a perfect couple.

"Introduce us," Wilma insisted.

"No," Jillian replied curtly.

"Oh, come on, Jillian. I've just got to meet him."

Jillian felt a lump growing in her throat. "Maybe some other time. He just started working here today and I don't want him to think I'm paying him to socialize with the customers."

Wilma turned her face to Jillian, a sly gleam in her eyes. "Is that the only reason, Jillian?"

She knows, Jillian thought. Somehow the woman knows that Linc Rider's presence is driving me plumb crazy.

Oh, Lordy. Was she that obvious?

Jillian was breathless. "Yes."

Wilma smiled. "Good. Then you won't mind if I take a second to invite him over to my place for dinner one night?"

"He eats with us," Jillian replied, wishing she could box the woman up and ship her to another continent. One with enough single men on it that she wouldn't ever think of Linc Rider again.

"Well, then," Wilma said, "consider this as a favor to you. I'll take him off your hands for one night. Maybe even two, if all goes well."

Jillian took back that last thought she'd just had of Wilma. Instead of sending her to another continent, Jillian wished she could ship the woman to another planet. Wilma Jenkins deserved to be in a world dominated by little green men who had one bulging eye in the middle of their foreheads. Jillian shrugged. "Go ahead."

Staring in Linc's direction, Wilma chewed down on the piece of gum in her mouth, causing it to make a popping sound. Then she strutted off to meet him.

Jillian's breath locked in her throat. She wanted to follow Wilma, to somehow stop her, but she couldn't think of one single way to accomplish that without looking like a complete idiot.

"Hi, there," Jillian heard Wilma say.

Linc's hammering stopped. "Hello."

"Jillian tells me you're her new hired hand."

"That's right."

"Well, I'm Wilma. I live just down the road."

"I'm Linc."

For several seconds Jillian didn't hear anything and she could just picture the two of them sizing each other up. She already knew Wilma liked what she saw. Undoubtedly, the same would hold true for Linc.

"How about coming to my place for dinner some night? I'm a good cook. But let me warn you, I like everything on the spicy side. How about you?"

"Spicy food's all right."

"Then how about tonight?" Wilma asked in a sultry tone of voice.

"Nope. Tonight's out of the question. I already have plans to play baseball with someone."

"Oh. Well, then, how about tomorrow night?"

"Look, Wilma, to be perfectly honest, I just started this job and I'm not real sure about anything just yet. But if I'm still here in a few days, I'll consider your invitation."

"Sure," Wilma answered, disappointment evident in her tone of voice. "Just give me a call, okay? I'm in the phone book."

"Will do," Linc replied with a certain pleasantness in his voice that Jillian didn't recall ever hearing before.

Still, her heart sang like a canary. He had refused Wilma's invitation. Well, not exactly refused. More like postponed it. But that was good enough for now.

Linc's hammering started up again. Within a second, Wilma reappeared at the checkout counter, paid Jillian for her carton of cigarettes, and then breezed out without further comment.

Sighing with relief now that the sultry-looking woman was gone, Jillian walked around the rows of shelves to where Linc was and found him squatting down, pounding in a long nail. She watched him as he finished the job and rose to his full height.

"That woman who just left, is she a friend of yours?" he asked, cocking his head to one side as he gazed over at her. He wiped his forearm across his mouth.

Jillian dug her hands into the pockets of her blue-jean skirt. She wished he hadn't done that. The simple gesture made her want to lick her dry lips. "Well . . . she's not exactly a friend. She comes in fairly often, though. Why?"

Grinning, Linc shrugged. "No reason."

"She's pretty, isn't she?" Jillian said. Using one hand, she lifted her long hair from the back of her neck so she could feel some fresh air there. Unconsciously, she nibbled on one corner of her bottom lip.

"Yeah, she's okay. Says she likes her food spicy."

"So I heard."

"But too much spice can upset a man's stomach."

"Yeah," Jillian replied. "I've heard that, too."

His grin widened. "Do you think I should take her up on her offer to cook me dinner?"

Jillian shrugged. "If you like a woman who implies she's as spicy as the food she cooks."

"Actually, I seldom compare food to a woman, if you know what I mean," Linc said, his gaze lingering on her lips.

"No, actually, I haven't the slightest idea what you mean," Jillian replied with a slow shake of her head. By now her stomach had turned to the consistency of warm butter. He had a look in his eyes that was capable of bringing her to a full boil. She knew she should turn and run at this point, but heaven help her, she didn't want to.

"Then come here and I'll show you," Linc drawled. And in the next instant, she found herself pulled into his strong arms. Then his full, sensuous mouth covered hers.

Chapter Five

Linc deepened the kiss. He had to. The woman was driving him wild. He wanted to feel every inch of her. She tasted pure and wholesome, and yes, just as sweet as the maple syrup she had served him at breakfast. Her soft, pliant lips trembled beneath his. His tongue sought to mate with hers, and she answered it with a hesitant shyness that made his stomach tighten in knots.

Tangling his hand in Jillian's hair, Linc tore his lips from hers and gently pushed her face against his chest. He held her there because he simply wasn't ready to release her just yet. Heaven help him, but she felt good in his arms. She felt right. He knew it was ridiculous of him to have such thoughts. If she knew who he was and his real reason for being here, she would hate him.

He wanted to hate her.

Linc heard Jillian's erratic breathing and knew she was every bit as shaken as he was by what had just happened between them. Trying his best to ignore the desire to hold her in his arms forever, he fought for control because, in that moment, that was what he told himself he needed more than anything. Even more than he needed her.

Liar.

He should have taken the redhead's offer. From the seductive looks she'd given him, no doubt she would have been willing to spice up more than just his dinner. She probably would have seasoned his whole night. And an "easy come, easy go" woman like her was just what he needed. But surprisingly, he hadn't even been tempted. That alone should have told him he was in big trouble.

Linc heard someone open the front door and enter the store. The sound prevented him from making another big mistake. Because for one fleeting moment there, he'd thought to whisper some sweet nothing to Jillian that he would've later regretted. Jillian, now looking totally perplexed by her own behavior, sprang from him in one quick motion.

"Oh, Lord," she mumbled, smoothing out her clothes. Then, without meeting his gaze, she whispered, "I never want this to happen again. Do you understand me?"

"Perfectly," Linc replied, standing in the middle of the aisle with his hands on his hips and watching as Jillian spun around and hurried to the front of the store to greet her customer. By now Linc's own emotional guards were back in place and he wasn't going to allow himself to reexperience the tender moments they'd just shared any more than she obviously was. Once, he told himself, was more than enough.

So what did it matter if for a few fleeting moments he'd realized that he'd have some regrets when leaving this place—this woman—behind? At least when the time came he wouldn't be leaving alone. His son would be going with him.

Right?

Right.

And reminding himself of that should have made him feel a whole lot better.

But this time, it didn't.

Linc picked up the hammer and another nail, placing the nail just so and then slamming the hammer down on its head, driving the metal into the wood, anchoring it. Once, twice... three times. Yeah... now he was beginning to feel a whole lot better.

Still shaken from the kiss, and by the very audacity of the man who had kissed her, Jillian stepped behind the check-out counter and stood in her usual place behind the cash register. Immediately recognizing the customer who had entered, she smiled. "Hi, Dan," she said. "What can I do for you today?" She hoped her voice sounded normal.

Dan Guillory and his wife owned a small farm just a mile up the road. They were a pleasant couple, good customers, and Jillian considered them her friends. Ordinarily Dan would have greeted Jillian with a smile. So when he didn't, her first guess was that he had witnessed her unladylike conduct of moments ago. Embarrassed that anyone had seen her, Jillian felt her face flame with color.

"Is your boy here, Jillian?" he asked, his voice sounding stressed.

Oh, for heaven's sake, what did he want with Eric? Of all the people in the world, her son was the last person she wanted informed about her earlier behavior. "Not right now, Dan," she heard herself saying in an unsteady voice. "Is there a problem?"

He shook his head in frustration. "Nah. It's just I went and pulled a muscle in my back yesterday and I can hardly walk. Unfortunately, I'm out of feed for my animals. I can't wait until Saturday morning when that high school kid comes in to help out. I need at least two sacks now."

So the source of his frown wasn't her behavior, after all, Jillian realized, feeling almost weak with relief. "Have you seen a doctor for your back?" she asked.

"Nah. My Becky wants me to. But I don't think it's necessary. I might go tomorrow, if it isn't any better."

Jillian came around the checkout counter and headed for the storeroom, where all the different kinds of feed were kept. "Look, pull your truck around to the side door and I'll load up as many sacks as you need."

"You can't be serious, Jillian. Those sacks must weigh . . . why, I bet they weigh forty pounds. I can't let you do that."

"I'm as strong as Eric. I know I can do it."

Dan was shaking his head. "No, you can't. And now that I think about it, those sacks would be too heavy for Eric, too. I'll just have to come back later."

Linc walked into view. "That won't be necessary," he said. "I can load them for you."

Dan looked at Linc, then over at Jillian as though to ask, "Who's he?"

But Linc didn't give her a chance to explain. "I'm the new hired hand. The name's Linc."

Dan didn't bother to hide his surprise. "Well, you don't say?" he replied.

"Just drive around to the side, show me what you want and I'll load them up," Linc said.

"Sure thing," Dan replied, slowly moving toward the front door.

When it shut behind him, Linc looked over at Jillian. "Who normally does the heavy lifting around here?"

"I do," Jillian replied. "Except for Saturday mornings, when a neighbor's seventeen-year-old son comes in for a few hours to help load the really heavy merchandise like feed and fertilizer. The farmers in the area usually wait until then. But other than that, I depend on Eric when I need help. Why?"

"*Why?* Because a few moments ago you were going to attempt something rather stupid."

"Oh, really?" Jillian replied, a hint of anger in her voice.

"That's right. You were going to attempt to lift those heavy sacks. What were you hoping to prove, that you're as strong as any man? Do you really think that anyone gives a damn about something so trivial?"

Immediately, Jillian gathered up her emotional guards. "Maybe they do. Maybe some people admire women who... who are hardy and as strong as an ox."

Linc looked her up and down. "Hardy... maybe. But as strong as an ox?" He caught her by the upper arm and squeezed lightly as though looking for muscle tone. "Hardly."

Jillian jerked her arm from his light grasp. "I don't have to prove anything to anyone. I've been running this store practically by myself for three years now and I've done just fine without your advice—or your help. I certainly can—and will—continue to do so."

Linc narrowed his eyes. "Just don't let me catch you trying to lift anything as heavy as a forty-pound sack of feed. That's my job from now on."

"And just who do you think will be doing it after you're gone?" Jillian asked.

Linc narrowed his gaze. "I have no idea. But until then, I'll do all the lifting. Would that be okay with you, boss?"

Now how was she supposed to think straight when he had those blue, blue eyes of his leveled on her face? "Perfectly."

His smile was haughty. "Good. At last we seem to understand each other." Then he spun on his heels and headed outside.

Minutes later Dan came back into the store to pay for his purchases. "I sure hope the new handyman works out for you, Jillian. Becky and I don't know how you do it alone."

"Eric is a big help," Jillian replied. "And so is Gram, when she's feeling well."

"I know Eric's a good kid and all. But that's just it. He's just a kid. You need someone in here who's strong, someone who can take charge if need be. What you need is a man around this place, Jillian."

"Dan, you know that times have been tough since Henry died and—"

"If I remember correctly, times were tough even before Henry died. And to be perfectly honest with you, at first I was really worried about your ability to keep this place going by yourself. But that's no longer the case. You've astounded me and everyone else in the area with the way you've handled things. Now it's just you that we're worried about. You can't keep going nonstop like you have for the past three years, Jillian. It isn't healthy. You have Eric to think about."

"I can't afford to hire someone permanently. At least, not just yet. Linc is temporary," Jillian said as the entrance door opened and Linc stepped inside. Their gazes locked. "He'll be gone in a few days."

The immediate electrical charge flowing between them could almost be felt. Clearing his throat, Dan looked from one to the other. "Well . . . yeah . . . whatever you say, Jillian," he replied. Then, using his right hand as support for his back muscles, he walked out.

By this time Jillian had turned her eyes away from Linc. But Linc stood in the same spot, his intense gaze still on Jillian. "I told Dan I'd follow him home and unload his truck, if that's okay with you."

Jillian couldn't bring herself to meet his stare again. "That's fine with me. I'm sure he would appreciate the help."

Linc walked out without further ado. Jillian turned toward the stove to check on lunch. She would have gladly done anything to keep herself from thinking about her new hired hand. He was impossible...arrogant...infuriating. He drove her crazy by simply being near. Even his kiss was unbearable to think about. He was handsome—and sexy—and wild.

And the total opposite of what she'd need in a man—if indeed she needed a man.

But, of course, she didn't, she quickly reminded herself. And she was getting tired of having everyone tell her differently.

Still, just thinking about the way his lips had felt and tasted on hers was enough to make her pulse pound. Never, ever, in her whole life had she felt so...so hungry for a man's touch.

And heaven help her, if she wasn't careful, she still could feel that way. But, thank goodness, she was quickly getting back in control.

Satisfied that her common sense was still intact, Jillian inhaled deeply. Then, turning around, she found Gram standing a few feet away, watching her.

"What's wrong, Jillian?"

"Nothing, Gram," she answered.

"For a second there, you looked worried."

Jillian shook her head. "No. No, I'm fine."

"It's that new helper you've hired, isn't it?"

Again, Jillian shook her head. "No. It's nothing."

Gram studied her for a few moments. "It *is* him, isn't it?"

Jillian nodded. "I guess so."

"I figured as much."

"He's a drifter, Gram."

"I can see that, Jillian, just by looking at him."

"Well, so can I," Jillian replied.

"Then that's all that either of us needs to say concerning him," her mother-in-law replied. "Besides, that's not the reason I came out here."

"Then what is it?"

"I noticed that the store wasn't all that busy during the morning. I think I can handle it for now. Why don't you go in to the back and rest for a while?"

Sighing deeply, Jillian walked to the front entrance, opened the door and glanced both ways down the highway. Finding both the road and the parking lot out front empty of any vehicles, she shut the door. "Well, I guess I could. That is, if you're sure you feel like staying up here by yourself."

"You know I enjoy helping out in the store," Gram said. "It makes me feel useful."

Jillian smiled. "You are useful, Gram. I couldn't handle any of this without you."

"I've been thinking a lot about that lately, Jillian. You've been like a daughter to me. God knows I loved my son, but Henry's gone. And it's time you started to think about yourself. You're still a young woman. You still have a long life ahead of you."

"I'm doing just fine like I am, Gram."

The older lady sat down in a rocker that had been placed behind the checkout counter years ago for her use. "Are you really?"

"We have a roof over our heads and food on the table."

Gram was shaking her head before Jillian had completed her sentence. "I'm not talking about that. I know you can run this store. You've done it. It's the other things in life that have me worried."

Confused, Jillian smiled. "What other things are you talking about?"

"I'm talkin' about finding yourself a husband, that's what," Gram stated matter-of-factly. "I think it's time you did."

"A husband?" Jillian repeated in surprise.

"That's right. Do you think I'm so old that I can't recall what a woman your age needs? Huh, well, I'll be damned."

"Gram . . ."

"I know. I know. I'm cursing again. But at my age, who cares? Now go on, Jillian, and get some rest. And while you're at it, put on some rouge and a bit of lipstick before coming back out front. And it wouldn't hurt for you to think about smiling more often, either. You have a lovely smile, Jillian."

For a moment, Jillian could only gape at her mother-in-law. What, she wondered, had gotten into the woman?

In fact, what had gotten into everyone? First off, there was Barney, who made no bones about what he thought she needed. Then there was Dan, who thought she needed help in the store. Then Linc, who thought she needed someone to do her lifting. And now Gram, who thought she needed—heaven forbid—a husband.

Walking toward the back, Jillian shook her head. *Rouge and lipstick, indeed!*

By early afternoon, Jillian was behind the checkout counter again. After eating lunch, Gram had gone to bed for her usual afternoon nap. Eric came in from outside at the same time that Linc did. They were talking and laughing together. But then they both quickly sobered when they saw Jillian.

"Is lunch ready yet?" Eric asked.

"It's been ready," Jillian answered. "Where have you been all morning, Eric?"

"After I picked up Mrs. Bramley's eggs, she asked if I'd feed her chickens. That took a while. Then I took out her garbage. Then she said it was a pretty day and asked me if I'd mind hanging out her wash on the clothesline out back." Eric's expression became distraught. "I didn't want to, but I said yes. But guess what happened?"

"What?" Jillian asked. A horrible picture visualized. She could see Eric breaking their neighbor's clothesline and sending the old lady's clean wash to the dusty ground.

"Wally and his brother drove by and honked at me. And when I looked over, Wally was killing himself laughing. I bet he goes and tells everyone on the team that I was hanging out old lady Bramley's underwear."

Jillian shook her head. "Wally is your best friend, Eric. He wouldn't say such a thing."

"Wanna bet?"

"So what if he does?" Linc chimed in.

"Then everybody's going to think I'm a sissy."

"Not if you don't let them," Linc continued.

"I don't approve of fighting," Jillian cut in.

Linc shifted his gaze to her. "I wasn't talking about fighting. I was talking about not letting them get the better of him." He dropped his eyes back to Eric. "The best thing for you to do is to own up to what you were doing and why you were doing it. Tell them you were helping Mrs. Bramley because she's sick."

"And you think that's going to make a difference? No way," Eric replied.

Linc could imagine his son being teased by the other kids his age for having done something nice for an old lady who'd needed help. And it angered him. "Then if that doesn't work, curl up your fist like this and—"

"Linc!" Jillian cried out.

Her voice stopped him in midsentence, which gave him the time he needed to get back in control of his temper. "I mean...well..." He faced Jillian. "Hell, he can't very well just sit there and let them pick on him."

"Fighting isn't the answer. And I can assure you that cursing isn't, either."

Linc grinned. "But sometimes it helps relieve the tension."

"However, it doesn't set a very good example of proper behavior for an eleven-year-old boy to follow," Jillian replied pointedly.

She was right. Which made him wrong, Linc summarized. Again. As much as he hated to think so, it seemed he had a lot to learn about being a father. Why did everything about being Eric's mother seem to come so naturally for her?

Being a good parent wasn't going to be as easy as he thought. There were all these rules to be taught. And examples to be set, not to mention the many decisions that were constantly being made in regard to another person's future happiness. And then, as if that weren't enough, there was always the guilt that seemed to accompany any mistakes in judgment that a parent might make. Like he felt now.

"Sorry, kid. Your mama's right. I must've lost my head for a moment."

Eric frowned. "Well, I agree with you, Linc. If Wally says one little thing about it, I'm gonna punch him in the nose."

"You will not do any such thing, Eric. Now do you hear me?" Jillian replied sternly.

Eric hung his head. "Yes, ma'am."

"And it's not that I don't understand the way you feel, Eric. It's just that fighting with your best friend isn't going to help anything. If I were you," she continued, a smile lifting the corners of her mouth, "I'd wait to see what happens. If—and only if Wally starts to tease you—then I'd remind him of what you saw him do last week that you haven't told anyone about. Remember when the two of you came in here and you were laughing . . . ?" she said, waiting for Eric to respond.

"Oh, yeah," Eric replied. "Now I remember. Yeah, that ought to do it. Wally doesn't want anybody to know about that."

"See," Jillian explained. "That's called compromise."

Linc coughed into his fist. "That's called blackmail," he said. Then he looked over at Eric and winked. "But I think it might work, kid."

"Yeah, I do, too," Eric responded.

After that, the three of them ate dinner. Then Eric went to clean his bedroom and Linc returned to his shelving.

By midafternoon Linc had finished repairing all the broken shelves. The total number: seven. Tomorrow he planned to climb the roof to see what repairs would be needed there.

For the most part, time had passed rather quickly while he'd worked. Still, he'd found lots of time for planning his future. And his future always included his son.

He had to have Eric. God, now that he'd seen him . . . and touched him . . . he wanted the boy—even more than he could ever have imagined. So maybe he wasn't the wisest of men. And maybe he didn't have all the answers. But surely even the best of fathers made mistakes. Sometimes, even big mistakes. But he wanted so badly to succeed for Eric, surely that was some sort of guarantee that he would. Wasn't it?

Yes. Yes, of course it was. He would do just fine, he told himself.

Better than Jillian?

Yes. No. Yes. Well, maybe not better. But certainly as good.

Which reminded him of something he'd almost forgotten—his promise to play baseball with Eric today. After glancing at his wristwatch, he began picking up his tools to put them away until tomorrow. Jillian didn't ask him any questions when he walked out at five o'clock, and he didn't volunteer any answers.

He found his son waiting for him at the picnic table, a ball and glove placed on the bench beside him. When Eric saw him, the boy jumped up and grabbed the glove and ball in one motion.

"Ready?" he asked hopefully, slipping the glove onto his left hand.

"Yeah, kid. Just give me a minute, okay?"

"Sure," Eric said, casually tossing the baseball deep into the pocket of his own glove.

Linc pulled off his T-shirt and tossed it onto the redwood table. "I've been looking forward to this all day."

Grinning, Eric replied, "Me, too."

"Got an extra glove?"

Eric's smile faded.

"Well, that's okay. My hands need a little toughening up."

"I won't throw too hard," Eric said.

Linc shook his head. "No. I want you to give it all you've got. If we're going to work on strengthening your skills, that's the only way."

Eric's grin was back. "Okay. You asked for it." Then, running close to a hundred feet from Linc, he turned and threw the ball as hard as he could to him.

Eric's baseball and Linc's flesh made a popping sound on contact. An immediate pain shot up Linc's arm. "Ouch!" he bellowed. "That's some arm you've got there, kid."

"Thanks. But are you all right?" Eric asked. "I didn't hurt you, did I?"

"No. I'm fine," Linc said, getting ready to pitch the ball back to Eric. "See if you can catch this."

It was a straight fastball and Eric caught it easily.

The exchange between the two continued for fifteen minutes. And Linc loved every minute of it. This was the way it should have been all along for him and Eric. Father and son. Together.

It wasn't like Eric not to be underfoot at this time of the day, Jillian thought, using a pink feather duster to remove the lint that had settled over the candy display. It was getting close to supper, and knowing him as she did, she knew he was always eager to know when his next meal would be served.

And Linc was missing, too. Of course, she wasn't concerned about him. The man could do what he pleased. It was just that she couldn't help wondering if Eric's lack of appearance had anything to do with Linc's disappearance.

Someone entered the store. After sighing loudly, Jillian glanced over and saw Barney Langford standing just inside the door, his angry eyes leveled on her.

"Hello, Barney. What can I do for you?" Jillian said, quickly deciding it was best for everyone concerned if she just pretended that the incident from last night was forgotten. She forced a smile. Still, she wanted something wide and solid separating the two of them and so she quickly slipped around the checkout counter.

"Where is he?" Barney asked point-blank.

"Who?"

"You know who I'm talking about. Where is he?"

"Now, look here, Barney, I don't want any trouble. If you've come here to start something, then just get out of here."

Smirking, Barney walked up to the counter and glared at her for what seemed like an eternity. Then suddenly he spun on his heels and headed for the cooler against the back wall. He pulled out a six-pack of beer, walked back to the front and slammed it down on the counter in front of Jillian. "Give me a pack of cigarettes, too," he growled.

Truly, Barney was pushing his luck with her. She knew she couldn't physically throw him out. He was too big for that. But she wasn't going to take his insults anymore. She got the cigarettes he wanted and placed them on the counter by his six-pack. "What else?" she asked in a cold voice.

He reached for her hand, but she was quicker. "Why don't you like me, Jillian? I like you."

"I do like you, Barney, as a friend. And as a friend, I'm telling you that you need to cut down on your drinking."

Suddenly, with the quickness of a snake, he reached out, grabbed her by the wrist and jerked her toward him. The corner of the countertop pressed against her stomach.

"Barney, let go of me."

"Where's your boyfriend?"

Jillian clenched her teeth together. "I told you, he's not my boyfriend. Now I'm warning you for the last time, let me go."

Jillian would never know if it was her determined expression or the sound of her voice that penetrated Barney's hard head. But something, somehow, seemed to register with him and he relaxed his hold. Immediately, Jillian stepped back. "Just get out of here. Right now, Barney. And don't come back in here unless you're sober."

Leaving behind the six-pack of beer he'd gotten from the cooler and also the cigarettes he'd wanted, Barney rushed for the door, almost as though he'd just discovered his life depended on it. Jillian breathed a sigh of relief. Moments later, she heard his motorcycle roar to life. Hot tears sprang to her eyes and that was when she realized how stressed out she'd become over the encounter. She reached for a tissue and was dabbing at her tears when she once more heard the entrance door open. Thinking it was Barney again, she froze.

Then Linc came into view. He strolled in, tucking his T-shirt into the waistband of his jeans.

Jillian turned away, not wanting him to notice that she was upset.

But she wasn't quick enough. In a second he was behind her, placing his hand on her shoulder and turning her around to face him. "Hey, what's the matter?"

"Nothing," she replied, her fake smile wobbling at the corners.

Searching her face for clues, he frowned. "You don't strike me as the type of woman who cries at the drop of a hat. Something's wrong."

His concern seemed so genuine, Jillian could almost have believed he cared, really cared about her.

Which was utterly ridiculous, and she knew it.

"Barney Langford came in again, and although I made him leave, he managed to upset me before doing so."

"What did the bastard do this time?"

"It was nothing, really. And I'm fine now," Jillian said, sniffing away the last of the tears. She wanted to put the whole mess behind her. Whatever had gotten into Barney was bound to pass soon. But even if it didn't, she felt certain that he now realized she wasn't going to tolerate his pathetic behavior any longer. He wouldn't come back into her store drunk. At least, not for a while.

So, if that was the case, why did she still feel like burying her face in Linc Rider's chest and bawling her eyes out? What would crying on his shoulder accomplish?

Nothing. Absolutely nothing.

He was so close that she could smell the earthy combination of sweat, dust and pure male. "If you wouldn't mind," she heard herself saying anyway, "I'd like to be held for just a moment."

Apparently he didn't mind at all, because in an instant she found herself wrapped in his arms. Encircling his waist, she placed the side of her face against his chest, right near his heart.

They didn't speak. Somehow they both knew they didn't have to. Jillian found the comfort she sought. And for a time, it didn't matter that her mother had abandoned her as a child, or that her husband hadn't really loved her as he should have. It didn't even matter that fate had made her into such a hardy woman on the outside, and such a vulnerable mess on the inside. Nothing mattered but the moment... the comfort she was being given... and Linc.

"Feeling better?" he asked, his fingers now gently combing through her hair.

All she could manage for him was a nod.

And all he did for the longest time was hold her against his hard, lean body as though she were the most precious thing in the whole wide world to him.

And for those few brief moments, she felt she was.

Chapter Six

Taking a deep breath, Jillian pulled away from Linc's arms and took a step back. "Thank you," she said in a very businesslike tone.

"No problem," Linc said, responding to the coolness he now sensed in her. After all, he *was* just doing his job, he told himself. She was the boss, and her request to be held by him was the same as her asking him to do a chore. He'd done it. No questions asked.

So what if holding her in his arms had felt so damned good that he'd fleetingly wished things could have been different between them? Things *weren't* different. She had Eric. And he wanted him. The two of them were on opposing sides. They were like oil and water. They simply didn't mix well, no matter how many times they came together.

Neither Linc nor Jillian had heard Eric approach from the rear of the store. "What's going on?" he asked, drawing their attention.

"Nothing," Jillian replied self-consciously, wiping her hands down the sides of her skirt. "I'll be closing up soon and getting supper on the table."

Disquieted, Eric looked from his mother to Linc, then back to his mother. Finally he blurted out, "It was my fault, Mom."

Jillian frowned. "What was your fault?"

"It was all my idea," he continued.

"What was?" Jillian asked.

"When we played baseball earlier. It was all my idea, not Linc's."

Jillian caught Eric by the shoulders and made him look at her. "What are you talking about, Eric?"

Eric suddenly fell silent.

"Well?" Jillian asked.

"Never mind. It's nothing," Eric said. "I'll wash up for supper." He turned to go.

"Not so fast, young man," Jillian replied.

Slowly, Eric turned around to face her, but glanced over at Linc. "I'm sorry, Linc. I thought...I thought she knew."

By now Jillian's heart was beating faster. "Knew what?" Her hands settled on her hips. "Okay, what's going on here?"

"Actually," Linc said, "playing baseball together was my idea. I offered and Eric said yes."

"When was this?" Jillian asked, her tone of voice curt and authoritative.

"I'd offered this morning. However, we didn't play until we both finished our jobs. That was about an hour ago."

Jillian was furious. She should have known that someone with the nickname of Easy wouldn't keep his word. "You promised me—"

"Do you think we could have this discussion just between the two of us—you and me?" Linc asked.

Surprised by his request, Jillian took a step back and then glanced down at Eric. "I'll talk to you about this later, young man."

"But, Mom..."

"No buts, Eric."

"Go on, kid," Linc added. "Do as your mama says."

"It's not his fault," Eric repeated. "It's mine."

"We'll talk about it later," Jillian repeated.

Distressed, Eric turned and walked back into the house.

As soon as the door closed behind him, Linc said, "Okay, let's have it."

Jillian faced him. "You promised me—"

"I did no such thing. You *ordered* me to stay away from Eric. And I intended to do just that. But this morning the two of us got to talking, and then one thing led to another. He said he wanted to help me with the repairs. I told him I didn't think that was such a good idea. He looked disappointed. So I made the offer about playing baseball later. If that offends you, well, I'm sorry. But to be perfectly honest, maybe it's time you took a good look at the needs of your son. Apparently since your husband died, you've been so wrapped up in what you think you need to be doing in order for you and Eric to survive that you can't see the sun for the clouds in your eyes. Eric doesn't have a father." Having to say that out loud really cost him. He took a deep breath before continuing. "And his mother is too damned busy working to spend much time with him anymore. The kid didn't just lose a father three years ago, he lost his mother, too."

She slapped him across the face. Hard. The cracking sound echoed throughout the quiet building.

They stared at each other. Then Jillian began to tremble and tears flooded her eyes. Her voice was barely above a whisper when she spoke. "Just who do you think you are coming into our lives like this and telling me what a lousy mother I am?''

The deep hurt that Linc saw in her eyes made him sick to his stomach. "I'm sorry. I didn't mean to make it sound like that," he said. In that moment he hated himself for what he'd just said to her.

Fighting back the tears, Jillian turned away. "But you're probably right," she admitted, placing her fingertips over her lips. "Oh, God, I don't know what came over me. I've never hit anyone in my life."

"Forget it," Linc said, wishing he would have a sudden lapse in memory. That agonizing look in her eyes from a moment ago was going to haunt him for a long time to come. Possibly forever. "Believe me, I deserved it."

"No," Jillian replied. "An act of violence is never deserved."

"If it's in self-defense, it is. And that's exactly why you did it. You were defending yourself against my attack."

"My behavior was inexcusable."

"So was mine," Linc replied. "Look, Eric and I just seemed to hit it off, okay? I know you think I'm a bad influence on him, and maybe you're right. I admit I've never won any blue ribbons for good behavior. But the point is that I'm not going to be around here long enough to influence anybody. So what's wrong if he and I play a little baseball? What can it hurt?"

Jillian took a deep breath. Had she really been that blind to Eric's needs? If so, Linc was right. It was time for a change. Somehow she was going to find a way to become more active in her son's life. In the meantime...

"Perhaps I did overreact," Jillian heard herself saying. "I suppose it wouldn't hurt anything for you and Eric to spend some time together. But I don't want him on your motorcycle. My father was killed on one of those things be-

FIND OUT **INSTANTLY** IF YOU GET UP TO 5 FREE GIFTS IN THE

LUCKY

CARNIVAL WHEEL

▼ `SCRATCH-OFF GAME!` ▼

Scratch off ALL 3 gold areas

YES! I have scratched off the 3 Gold Areas above. Please send me all the gifts for which I qualify. I understand I am under no obligation to purchase any books, as explained on the back and on the opposite page. 215 CIS ANDH
(U-SIL-R-01/94)

NAME

ADDRESS   APT.

CITY   STATE   ZIP

THE SILHOUETTE READER SERVICE™: HERE'S HOW IT WORKS

Accepting free books places you under no obligation to buy anything. You may keep the books and gift and return the shipping statement marked "cancel". If you do not cancel, about a month later we will send you 6 additional novels, and bill you just $2.24 each plus 25¢ delivery and applicable sales tax, if any.* That's the complete price, and—compared to cover prices of $2.75 each—quite a bargain! You may cancel at any time, but if you choose to continue, every month we'll send you 6 more books, which you may either purchase at the discount price...or return at our expense and cancel your subscription.

*Terms and prices subject to change without notice. Sales tax applicable in N.Y.

fore I was born. And there's nothing you or Eric can say that's going to change my mind on that subject."

"Fair enough," Linc said.

Jillian hesitated, not knowing what to say next. Linc seemed to be at a loss for words, too.

"Uh...if you'll excuse me, it's almost time for me to close the store," Jillian said, taking a step in the direction of the cash register.

Linc captured her arm. "Look...if you ever need someone to talk to, I'm a pretty good listener." Now why had he said that? Hadn't he dished out enough mush for one day?

What was he trying to prove? he wondered. That he was one of the good guys? Hell, he knew himself better than that. He'd come here for one reason and one reason alone. To take back his son. And by doing so, he was going to destroy this woman's world. And one thing was for certain. In the old Western movies that he watched on late-night television, a character like himself wouldn't have been the one wearing the white hat.

That sick feeling was back in the pit of his stomach.

Jillian gave a reluctant nod. "I'm okay—but thanks just the same for the offer."

"Sure," he replied, standing there like an awkward teenager. What in the hell was happening to him? He'd never been bashful in his life. Not even as a kid. Still, feeling almost too clumsy to move, he just stood there with his hands tucked into the back pockets of his jeans and watched her walk away.

He felt as though he were on a roller-coaster ride. One minute he wanted to take Eric and run from this place. The next minute he wanted to stay right where he was—forever. A couple of times during the day, he'd even found himself wondering what it would have been like if Jillian had been his wife and Eric their son. Would his life really have been as easy and as fulfilling as his imagination had pictured?

Jeez ... would you listen to me? Linc thought, giving himself a sudden mental jolt. More mush, only this time it was stirring around in his head. He and Eric would be a family. Just the two of them. Jillian wasn't a needed part.

Dream on, the nagging voice inside him said. *Do you really think that you're going to be able to take Eric from here and he won't ever want to see his mother again? Come on. Surely you can't be so blinded by your own selfish needs that you don't see the strong bond between them? You even admitted it to yourself earlier. So face the truth now. Eric isn't going to just go away with you like you originally thought, and you know it.*

Maybe not yet, Linc argued back. But given enough time, he might.

Might?

Linc clenched his teeth. Eric *would,* he growled to himself. Then, spinning around on his heels, he rushed out through the same door he'd used when loading Dan Guillory's feed. He needed to be alone for a while. Those nagging doubts of his were becoming a total nuisance. They made him feel uneasy. And yes, dammit, scared, too. Maybe things wouldn't work out like he'd planned, after all. And that really frightened him. Because Linc Rider had never been scared of anything in his life. Until now.

But just the thought of losing the one person in this whole world to whom he had any connection was terrifying. He couldn't just give up without a fight!

And there was no use in his turning to Jillian for help. He was twenty-four hours too late for that. Maybe if he had leveled with her from the beginning, she might have understood—maybe even helped him, he told himself, though he didn't really believe that for one moment. When he'd walked into her store for the first time, she'd formed an immediate opinion of him, and it hadn't changed since. To her way of thinking, he was bad news and she wanted her son as far away from his influence as possible. Given any excuse at all, she'd be more than happy to send him packing—pronto. If she learned the truth about him now, the shock would only blow her mind completely. She'd panic, no doubt about it. *And* call the police. And then she'd use the legal system to force him from their lives.

And then he'd be alone, again, without his son. Without anyone.

So what's the answer, Rider?

At the moment, he didn't have a clear one. But he'd think of something soon. He had to. Because now that he'd found his son, turning his back and just walking away was impossible.

Unless, of course, he became convinced that Eric was better off without him. Because his son's welfare was the most important thing of all.

He couldn't help but wonder what Jillian would think of him if she knew his true feelings for Eric. Would she still consider him such a bad influence?

After closing the store, Jillian counted out the money she'd taken in for that day and registered the amount in the ledger she kept in a safe-deposit box under the counter. According to her tally, today's profit had been small.

However, she thought, the same certainly wasn't true where her emotions were concerned. Several times during the day, her feelings had rallied together to throw her off balance. And on every occasion that she could recall, Linc Rider had had something to do with it.

She should have listened to her common sense and sent him away first thing this morning. But, oh, no, not her. She

was too stupid. Why, she'd even enjoyed fixing him breakfast. And when she'd offered him seconds and he'd accepted, she'd actually been flattered that he liked her
cooking.

What an idiot she was. The man had probably been so
hungry, he would have eaten mud pies, had she served them.

But she had been flattered. Good Lord, was she really
that lonely? Maybe Gram was right. Maybe she did need to
find herself a husband.

Wouldn't having a husband who helped out in the store
give her more time to spend with Eric?

No, she reminded herself. It wasn't a husband she needed.
She just needed help. Good, dependable help. Someone she
could trust. Someone who wouldn't demand top wages.
Someone like...

Like Linc Rider.

No, not like him, she argued back. He worked for cheap,
all right, but could she trust him? Depend on him?

Uh-uh. His type never stayed long in one place.

And besides, what did she really know about him? *That
his kisses were heaven?* Nothing. Absolutely nothing. For all
she knew, he could be a common thief. Trusting him could
easily wind up being the biggest mistake she ever made.

No...she simply refused to consider Linc Rider as a
possible answer to any of her problems. She might have
agreed to allow him and Eric to practice baseball, but that
was as far as his involvement in their lives would go. As he'd
said, he wasn't going to be around long enough to change
anything.

Jillian had supper on the table within thirty minutes of
having closed the store. After grace was said, Gram suggested that someone turn on the television so she could
watch the local weather news. Eric got up, pressed the on
button and then waited for the picture to appear. When it

did, the voice came on, too, and he adjusted the sound according to Jillian's wishes before returning to his seat.

Before long, the meteorologist from the nearest TV station was predicting an eighty percent chance of rain for south central Louisiana by late tomorrow afternoon. Eric thought that meant he wouldn't have to water the garden after supper, but Jillian assured him otherwise. Linc said he would try to repair some of the leaks in the roof before the thunderstorms got started. Gram said he had better be careful when walking around up there, "'cause it was steep." Her late husband had once fallen from the very top and had broken his leg in three places. Linc inquired about the details of the accident, and much to everyone's surprise, by the time the conversation was over, so was supper.

Jillian gathered up all the dishes and carried them to the sink. This time Linc didn't offer to help her in the kitchen, which was for the best, she told herself. Instead, he followed Eric outside. It wasn't too long afterward that she heard his motorcycle roar to life. After hesitating only a moment, she hurried to the back door and glanced out. Eric came up at the same time.

"Did I hear a motorcycle?" Jillian asked.

"It was Linc," Eric said. "He left."

"Where's he going?"

Eric shrugged. "I don't know. He said he had to check on a friend."

"Oh," Jillian replied. "Then he's coming back."

Again, Eric shrugged. "He didn't say. But I sure hope so."

"Eric, I think you should know that a man like Linc Rider doesn't ever stay in one place for very long."

"I know. He's traveled all over the place. Even to Germany."

Jillian could hear the admiration in Eric's voice. "That's not what I meant. The reason he doesn't stay long in one place is because he doesn't have any roots anywhere. No family."

"How do you know?" Eric asked.

"I just do."

"He could stay here. Couldn't he?"

"No, he can't do that. And he wouldn't want to anyway. That's the point I'm trying to make. You must understand, Eric. He doesn't *want* to belong anywhere. He likes being a loner."

"I bet he doesn't. I bet if we offer him to stay here, he would."

Jillian could see the disappointment in her son's eyes. She hated having to disillusion him, but he would have to face the truth sooner or later. "I know you like him, Eric. That's why I've decided that the two of you can spend some time together." She ran her fingers through the front of her son's hair. "Just don't be surprised if we wake up one morning and find he's gone away during the night without even saying goodbye. Okay?"

"Okay. But I know he wouldn't do that."

Frustrated, Jillian took a deep breath. "I'm going to take a bath."

"May I watch TV?"

"For a while, Eric. But don't you have baseball practice tomorrow?"

He nodded. "At eight-thirty in the morning. Keith's mom is going to bring and pick up."

Jillian started walking toward the bathroom. "Then I think you should be in bed by ten o'clock."

Once again, Eric nodded in agreement and, turning up the volume on the television, plopped down on the floor to watch his favorite program.

Jillian began filling the bathtub. After pinning her hair up and opening a new bar of soap, she stepped into the already ankle-deep warm water. Leaning forward, she adjusted the faucet for a stronger flow of water, then, after a while, slipped back and submerged as much of her body as she could. She'd had a hard day—well, mentally, anyway—and needed this quiet, soothing time to herself to get her thoughts—and her emotions—back in order. Shutting her eyes, she concentrated on relaxing her tired muscles.

Was he coming back?

Her eyes sprang open. *He* was not someone she even wanted to think about and she chastised herself for allowing him to slip through the guard she had erected against her having any thoughts of him. *He* was the reason she'd had such a mentally exhausting day in the first place.

Was it only yesterday that he'd walked into her store? From the wear and tear on her emotions, it seemed more like decades ago.

If only she could understand her reaction to him. But so far, it was impossible. One minute she was leery of his character, the next she was allowing him to spend time with her son. One minute she wanted him gone from their lives, the next she wished he'd hold her in his arms forever. Undoubtedly her emotions were in a contradictory state of mind. A total mess. She had to regain control of herself.

And she would, she told herself, making a promise not to think of Linc Rider again while she was *trying* to relax in the tub. On guard this time, she shut her eyes with renewed determination.

Linc zipped down the highway toward Pine Creek. He'd driven to the state park and used the showers that were provided for the overnight campers. Now he was anxious to get back. It was as though he was heading home after having been gone away for too long. He knew it didn't make any sense, this feeling he had. But, dammit, he couldn't help it.

It was Eric, he knew. He wanted to be near him. The boy was his future.

But nothing was ever free. He was going to have to pay a high price, even for his own son. Because no matter what he told himself, hurting Jillian was going to bother him. A lot.

Why did he feel so responsible for her? Was it because she was Eric's adoptive mother? Yes ... that had to be it. And any tender feelings that he'd had for her since arriving were all relative to and confused with his feelings for his son!

Now that made sense. Actually, it was so simple that a moron could have understood it, Linc thought as he drove up to the backyard. He killed the engine and then pushed his motorcycle to the same spot along the outdoor kitchen that he had used for parking the night before.

The night was hot and humid. And as he headed for his sleeping bag, Linc felt it clearly when perspiration began dripping down the middle of his back. Before entering the outdoor kitchen, he glanced toward the house and saw it was dark inside. But he noticed when the blue-checked curtain in one of the windows facing him dropped closed. That particular window, he figured, was probably in Jillian's bedroom.

Had she been waiting up to see if he'd return?

That thought caused a heated rush through his body. His loins tightened and the palms of his hands began to sweat.

Southern nights and Southern women. What was a sane man to do when the heat from the first was enough to drive him mad, and the hots for the other was enough to help accomplish the damned mission?

Nothing, his inner voice chimed in. *There's absolutely nothing you can do. It's apparent she's already in your blood.*

Like hell, he told himself as he headed for his bedroll. Aggravated, he pulled off his T-shirt and threw it down on the floor near his duffel bag. Next he pulled off his shoes and socks. Finally, he removed his jeans. In no time at all he was lying on his back with only his jockeys covering his body.

He was hot. Damned hot. Again.

Jillian slept late. Therefore, getting breakfast on the table and the store open at its usual time was enough to start her day at a hectic pace. Add the cancellation of Eric's ride to baseball practice because of sickness, and Jillian was ready to pull her hair out. Gram offered to help, but Jillian knew her mother-in-law didn't like working alone in the store first thing in the morning when most of the deliveries were being made. Somehow, she'd find a way to get Eric to practice.

Linc came in late for breakfast and missed that discussion altogether. From the moment he'd walked into the kitchen, Jillian somehow knew he'd seen her watching him through her window last night, and avoided eye contact with him. But after eating, he'd walked up behind her to thank her for the meal and, when she'd turned around to answer him, their gazes had locked. And from the amused twinkle in his, she knew she was correct in her assumption.

When Jillian unlocked the store, she saw two delivery trucks were already in the parking lot, waiting on her. Before she had a chance to open the register, three customers had walked in.

Early-morning customers were generally in a hurry to get to work. They seldom wanted a cup of the freshly brewed coffee when Jillian offered it to them. So she didn't bother with immediately putting on a kettle of water to boil for coffee. Instead, she went to the register.

The last customer had just driven away when Eric showed up.

"Who's gonna take me to practice, Mom?"

"Oh, Eric, I forgot all about that."

"Mom . . ."

"I know, I know. I'll think of something," she said.

Just then Linc walked in. "Look, I've been up on the roof and I'm going to need some extra material in order to get it patched up. I can't very well bring back supplies on my motorcycle. So I guess you'll have to let me use that old pickup I saw parked in the garage out back."

Jillian sighed. "That old pickup just happens to be our only means of travel, Linc."

"Does it run?"

"Of course it runs. What good would it be to us if it didn't run?"

"None that I can see. It's an old model, but not old enough to be worth anything as an antique."

"Well, I *guess* not," Jillian said, feeling almost offended by his remarks. "Old Yeller is only about thirteen years old, I'll have you know."

"Old Yeller?"

Eric grinned for the first time. "Yeah, that's what Mom calls the truck. 'Cause it's yellow—and old," he added, looking from his mother to his friend. "Right, Mom?"

Jillian didn't bother to answer him. Instead she sighed. "Well, I'm going to need to use Old Yeller this morning, too. Eric's got to get to practice."

Linc hesitated a moment, then shrugged. "That's an easy one. I'll just drop him off on my way to the lumberyard and then pick him up on my way back. That way you don't have to leave at all."

It made sense, Jillian told herself. Perfect sense, actually. So why was she hesitant?

"Well . . . I don't know. I mean, it's all so sudden."

Linc stood there, shifting his weight from one foot to the other. "It's just an offer to help out, Jillian. The decision's all yours to make."

Whenever he said her name, which wasn't often, thank goodness, she felt as though his voice vibrated through her.

She looked down at Eric just as he glanced up at her. Giving her a cocky little grin, he said, "What's wrong, Mom? You think he's gonna kidnap me or something?" Then he laughed.

Jillian shook her head. "No, Eric. That's not it."

"Then what is?" he asked.

"Look, kid, maybe it's better if we just forget it. Your mama can take you to baseball practice. I'll go to the lumberyard when the two of you get back." He faced Jillian. "Is that simple enough for you?"

Jillian felt like such a jerk. The guy was only trying to help. And now, because of Eric's silly remark, he probably thought that she didn't trust him. "That won't be necessary," she finally said. "I'd really appreciate it if you could get Eric to practice."

"Great!" Eric squealed. He ran off to get his hat and glove.

Jillian cleared her throat. "Look, Eric was just joking earlier...and well...I just want you to know that I feel Eric is safe with you."

Linc tightened his jaw. "You should never trust strangers, Jillian."

"What exactly are you saying?"

He moved in closer, close enough to gather her in his arms, if that had been his intent. "Don't," he repeated slowly, "ever trust a stranger."

"Like you?" she whispered, her eyes widening with curiosity and suspense.

"Like me," he answered.

"I'm ready, Linc," Eric said, storming up to them.

Still staring into Jillian's eyes, he said, "Then let's go, kid."

"Wait," Jillian cried out, grabbing hold of his arm. "Tell me the truth."

Linc dropped his eyes to where she held him, then lifted them back up to hers. Suddenly he relaxed his stance and smiled. "He'll be fine."

Jillian tightened her grip. "Are you sure?"

"He's in good hands, I tell you," Linc replied.

"Then you're holding my life in your hands," Jillian replied, a lump forming in her throat.

"I'll try to remember that," Linc said, his blue eyes boring into hers.

She released him, and he and Eric went out the door as a customer was coming inside. Telling herself to relax, Jillian forced a smile.

No way was she going to allow some silly fear to overrule her better judgment. Linc had been pulling her leg. Eric *was not* in any kind of danger. And that was that. Period.

Chapter Seven

The next hour and a half passed quickly. Jillian was busy with customers and only glanced once at the clock on the wall behind her to see how late it was getting. She chose to ignore the slight twinge of apprehension that oozed down her spine. Eric and Linc *would* be home soon.

In spite of what she was telling herself, when she heard the sound of Old Yeller's engine, she wasn't surprised at the amount of relief that swept over her.

Within a few minutes Eric came running inside. "Guess what, Mom?" he said breathlessly.

Jillian shook her head. It didn't matter how many times she told Eric to come into the store quietly, he always forgot when he had something exciting to tell her. "What, Eric?" Jillian replied, amused. She looked up when Linc entered, her smile still on her face.

"Linc helped my coach with practice."

She glanced down at her son. "He did what?"

"He helped my coach. You know," Eric added, "by throwing balls to us and pitching to us so we could get some extra batting practice in. It was neat."

As her smile faded slightly, Jillian gazed up at Linc. He shrugged. "It was something to do while I waited."

"Since you had so much time on your hands, you could have checked on your friend to see if he'd come home yet," Jillian said.

"You mean my friend Hal?" Linc asked.

"Yes, of course."

"Well, as a matter of fact, I did check on him."

"And?" Jillian asked.

"And he still hasn't come home," Linc replied.

"Does that mean you're not leaving?" Eric asked.

"Not yet," Linc replied.

Jillian placed her arm around Eric's shoulders and then looked again in Linc's direction. "Well, I'm sure Eric's coach was grateful for the help."

"Yeah, he seemed to be," Linc said in a casual tone of voice. "As a matter of fact, he said that I was more than welcome to assist him any time I felt like it."

"I was team mom once," Jillian pointed out. For a moment, she'd almost felt envious of the time Linc had spent with Eric and his friends. But then, she quickly reminded herself, if she had nothing better to do than drive around the countryside all day long like Linc Rider did, she'd have had time to help with Eric's team, too.

"I don't remember that," Eric replied.

"Well, it was years ago," Jillian said, hurt by the knowledge that it had been such a long time since she had taken part in Eric's life that he didn't even remember. "And you were very young."

Eric's features became animated. "Maybe next year you could do it again."

Jillian smiled tentatively. "Maybe so."

Linc cleared his throat. "Well, now that I've gotten the supplies to start mending the roof, I'd better get to it before it starts raining. On the way home, I noticed the clouds were already gathering."

Home? Jillian thought.

Had he used the word *home?*

A weakness settled in the pit of her stomach. "Eric, see if Gram needs anything. If she doesn't, check on Mrs. Bramley. I haven't seen her today. Make sure she's aware that we're supposed to have thunderstorms in the area by this afternoon."

"Okay," Eric said, trotting off.

After watching her son disappear through the doorway leading to the house, Jillian turned around and saw Linc going out the front entrance. Alone for the first time since she'd opened up for business, she decided to make a fresh pot of coffee. Then she prepared lunch.

At noon, Jillian went outside and yelled up to Linc that it was time to eat. From the rooftop, he yelled down that he wanted to continue patching up as many of the leaks as he could before the rain got started. She, Gram and Eric ate without him.

After lunch, the weather continued to deteriorate and by two o'clock the wind gusts were so strong they weren't only picking up leaves and dust and litter from the ground, but the force was enough to blow down lawn chairs that were on the front porch of the store, as well as scatter the few empty cardboard boxes that were stacked in a bend out back. Lightning that had once been at a distance now sliced through the sky overhead. Eric and Gram joined Jillian at the front of the store.

"Has Linc come down from the roof?" Jillian asked.

Eric shook his head. "I don't think so, Mom."

"I'm sure he will soon," she said, walking to the front door and looking out. Seeing the lawn chairs on the ground, she hurried outside to get them.

Eric met her at the entrance as she was coming back inside. "Maybe I ought to go look for him."

"No, Eric. He's a grown man. He'll be in when he thinks it's time."

"But, Mom . . ."

Again there was a flash of lightning, and then a tremendous burst of thunder followed. Jillian shivered. "Absolutely not, Eric. It's too dangerous out there."

Eric looked terrified. "But...but what if lightning strikes Linc?"

"It won't," Jillian said, but there was just a hint of uncertainty in her voice.

"It might."

"It won't, Eric."

"Please, Mom, let me go find him."

Jillian, too, was fighting a rising panic. Why hadn't Linc come inside, for heaven's sake? Anyone with good sense could see how dangerous the weather outside was becoming.

Finally, moved by Eric's pleadings—as well as her own worried thoughts—Jillian announced that she was going outside to get Linc.

The gusting wind—she estimated its force at about forty to fifty miles per hour—whipped at her face and clothing, and it took every ounce of her strength to place one foot in front of the other. She looked around the grounds to see if Linc was anywhere within her view, but he wasn't. She tried yelling his name, but the wind tossed away the sound of her voice. She looked up, hoping to see him on the edge of the roof, getting ready to come down, but he wasn't there, either.

Really worried now, she pushed her windblown hair away from her face as heavy raindrops began smacking down on the rooftop and on the hard, dry ground surrounding her. The merciless drops stung her flesh, but Jillian knew this was just a preface for what was still to come. Undoubtedly, an even harder downpour would be upon the area soon.

Suddenly a crackle of lightning just to the south of her ripped through the turbulent sky, immediately followed by a roar of thunder.

More than anything else, Jillian loathed stormy weather. As a child, she had been frightened by it. As an adult, she always kept indoors and tolerated it. But if she were to be totally honest with herself, she knew she'd have to admit that she was still afraid.

But for this moment, she needed to continue lying to herself. It was the only way for her to keep a cool head— and, if need be, to find the guts to climb up to the rooftop to find Linc. And somehow, she just knew that was going to be her fate.

A shiver ran down her spine. Fate or no fate, she was scared. Heights weren't exactly a thrill a minute for her, either. In fact, in this kind of weather, the only thrill she could think of was being indoors, with both of her feet planted firmly on the floor.

Thinking that Linc had probably placed the ladder against the back of the building, she hurried in that direction. Her flared denim skirt whipped between her legs and acted like a binding rope that pushed against her efforts to rush forward. Quickly rounding the corner of the house, a sudden strong gust of wind whirled beneath her skirt, causing it to puff out around her. She pushed at the denim fabric, trying to get it back down.

Finally, she found the ladder on the west side of the house. Apparently it had been blown down to the ground, because a part of it had fallen over a nearby azalea bush and had broken several of its branches. Within a tenth of a second Jillian realized why Linc hadn't come inside.

He was stranded on the roof.

Jillian jerked her gaze upward, hoping to see Linc waiting to be rescued. Disappointed when she didn't see him, she began to struggle with the ladder, trying to lift it back into place against the house. Her insides were shaking.

Constantly having to fight the hounding wind, Jillian steadied the ladder and then tried making sure it was secure. Not having any luck, she gave up and began to climb anyway. There was no time to waste. But like an old soldier determined to win today's battle, the force of the wind pounded against her every effort, seemingly unfeeling to the number of casualties it swept along with it. Linc's life. Her life. Indeed, it would probably have gladly claimed them both, if she had allowed it.

But she wouldn't, Jillian thought. Hanging on to the ladder by squeezing the support frame so tight her fingers and knuckles looked bloodless, she defied the wind. Still determined to be the victor of what seemed an endless battle with nature, she took one step at a time, halting a moment after each one to regain her balance—and her courage—before continuing. Once, a gust of wind was so powerful that Jillian had to press her body in close to the ladder to keep from being blown away. But then the ladder itself lifted away from the house, as though her extra weight didn't even make a difference. For a moment she feared the worst, but once the ladder settled back down, she took a couple of deep breaths and found the courage to continue. Slowly, she made her way higher... and higher.

Lightning crackled once more through the sky, causing Jillian to cringe. The explosion of thunder that immediately followed apparently ruptured a huge hole in the heavens and the downpour Jillian had expected to come at any minute suddenly began to fall to the earth in thick, angry sheets that nearly blinded her.

She took two more steps up and found herself at the top of the ladder, her eyes half-closed to protect them from the rain. Grabbing the edge of the roof with one hand, she held on to its security. Her heart was pounding as she thrust her weight forward, trying to get as much of her body onto the solid roof as she could. She succeeded from her waist up. She rested for a moment, then lifted her head to gaze around. She didn't see anyone.

What was she going to do? Just wait here to see if Linc suddenly showed up? She could hardly do that.

Obviously, she needed to think. If only her brain waves had more order to them. But under the circumstances, they didn't.

Another wind gust rocked the ladder beneath Jillian and she lost her footing. Struggling to regain her balance, she clawed at the coarse shingles covering the roof. Her feet were in a kind of war dance with the ladder as she tried desperately to regain control. But she sensed rather than felt when the ladder fell to the ground beneath her. Pure terror shot through her body, nearly paralyzing her efforts to breathe.

Oh, God! She was half on and half off the roof.

Worse, she was now stranded like that.

Linc watched the downpour of rain from inside the outdoor kitchen. He'd just made it down from the roof in time to get his motorcycle into the garage next to Jillian's pickup, but there hadn't been enough for him to go back for the ladder he'd left against the side of the house.

He'd really cut it close this time.

He would probably have worked even longer mending those leaks, but that last flash of lightning while he'd still been up on the roof had been just a bit too close for comfort. But now that his motorcycle was safe from any damaging winds and he was, too, for that matter, Mother Nature had his blessing to unleash her fury upon them.

He was disappointed, however, because he'd wanted to spend some of this unexpected time off with Eric. But instead, he'd become so involved with repairing the leaks in the roof that he'd waited too long before coming in from the storm and now, unless he wanted to get drenched, he'd have to wait out the storm alone.

Biting down on a toothpick he'd found in the pocket of his white T-shirt, he leaned against the doorframe, his thumbs hooked into the front pockets of his jeans, and watched the earth being renewed. Every now and then a gust of wind pushed the heavy rain inside the opening where he stood and he had to step back to avoid getting wet. Nonetheless, as indifferent as he was to the thunderstorm's fury, he always returned to his original position of being a casual observer.

He sure hoped that he'd mended most of the leaks in the roof and that Jillian wasn't having to run around putting pails under water dripping from the ceiling. Otherwise, she might not be inclined to serve him supper. And after having gone without food since breakfast, he was getting hungry. As a matter of fact, he was starving.

But more important, he wanted Jillian to be pleased with the work he'd done for her so far—not that he cared to analyze the reason he felt that way. Especially when he *did* have better things to do with his time. For instance, he could plan his and Eric's future together.

Now, that was something well worth his time.

A few moments later Linc was mostly daydreaming when his attention was suddenly drawn to the figure of a boy running toward him. Before he could even move from the doorway, Eric ran right up to him and began pulling on his arm. "Linc! You've got to come quick—hurry. It's my mom. She's stuck on the roof. Hurry—please," he continued hysterically.

"What?" Linc replied, shaking his head to clear it. *Jillian on the roof?*

"Hurry, Linc." Eric took off in a run, then came back and jerked impatiently on Linc's arm. "Come on..." he said. "Follow me."

Without asking any more questions, Linc dived into the rainstorm, running behind his son.

Eric led the way to the side of the building, stopped and pointed upward. "It's Mom," he yelled, though the storm almost drowned out his voice.

Linc gazed in the direction Eric gestured. Exactly what he'd expected to find wasn't clear to him, but when he looked up, he saw the bottom half of what he thought was a female body hanging from the roof in a most precarious way.

The situation looked serious and Linc knew any questions he had would have to wait until later.

He turned to Eric and found him struggling to lift the heavy ladder that had fallen to the ground. Hurrying to help him, Linc glanced up again and saw that Jillian was on the brink of falling. Realizing there wasn't time for a brilliant rescue operation, he dropped the ladder and moved under her. Cupping his hands around his mouth, he yelled, "Jillian, I'm going to catch you when you fall." He waited a moment, then yelled again. "Can you hear me, Jillian? I'm going to catch you."

Somehow Eric had managed to place the ladder against the wall and now Linc helped him secure it next to Jillian. He saw when she reached back to try to grab hold of it. Instead, she bumped the support board. Then everything began to happen so fast that Linc didn't have time to think. Suddenly her body swung to the right and she screamed. Then she was plunging toward the ground. The next thing he knew, he'd caught her in his arms, but the suddenness of her extra weight caused his own feet to slide out from under him and both of them landed on their backs.

Sopping wet, with their hair plastered down the sides of their heads, they took deep breaths and stared at each other. After a couple of seconds, Linc sat up. Dazed, he felt an anger building inside him that he couldn't control. *She could have died.* "Are you crazy?" he yelled at her. "What in the hell were you doing up there, anyway? You could've been hurt." He quickly looked her over. "Are you hurt?"

"I—"

"She was looking for you," Eric cut in when his mother seemed at a loss for words. His hair, too, was wet and plastered down the sides of his head. "We thought you were still on the roof."

For what seemed an eternity, Linc just stared at Jillian. Then, without further comment, he began to examine her more closely while the rain continued to splatter down around them. His hands gently but firmly checked for injuries.

"I—I'm okay," Jillian said.

"You sure?" he asked, bringing his face to within inches of hers.

She nodded. "Yes, I'm sure," she insisted. "I'm not hurt. Just...just shaken, I think." Her hand went to her face.

That was when Linc saw the ugly scratches on her forearm. He immediately lifted her other arm and found it to be in the same condition. "You're bleeding," he said.

"Huh?" Jillian said, sounding amazed. "But I don't feel anything."

"That's because you're still numb with shock," he replied. Standing, he lifted her into his arms. "Let's get her inside," he said to Eric.

Rain was still coming down heavily, but the danger from the intense lightning and thunder that had ruled over the area for a while had since moved off to the east, which was a typical weather pattern for south central Louisiana. Soon the rain would probably stop, the water would quickly drain away, and everyday life in the area would resume its normal mode.

Eric held open the back door to the house so Linc could carry his mother inside. They were in the kitchen now and Linc seated Jillian in a chair at the kitchen table. He began to reexamine her injuries. "Anything else hurting you?"

"No," she replied. "Nothing." She was beginning to shake.

"It must have been those damned shingles that rubbed the skin off your arms like this. My God, didn't you feel anything?"

"I—I guess I was too busy just trying to hang on," she replied.

"Eric, get your mama a blanket," Linc said, when he noticed she was trembling even more.

Eric hurried off to do as he was bid. He came back with a colorful crocheted afghan and placed it around his mother's shoulders. "Mom, Gram is in the store. I'm gonna go and tell her we found you and that you're all right."

Jillian nodded and Eric rushed away.

"You're pale," Linc said, kneeling in front of her with a warm cloth he'd dampened at the sink. After adjusting the lightweight blanket around her shoulders, he wiped her face and then very carefully wiped away the debris from the cuts on her arms. Afterward he stood, studied her for a moment and then walked back to the sink to dampen the cloth so he could begin the procedure all over again. "Do you have a first-aid kit?"

"Yes," she said in a low voice.

Having momentarily turned his attention to the task at the kitchen sink, Linc sensed something wrong with her and immediately cut his eyes back in her direction. "Are you okay?" he asked, hastily wringing out the cloth.

"Uh-uh," she said.

"Jillian, are you feeling weak?"

"A little."

"Do you want to lie down?"

"That would be nice," Jillian replied in a voice that lacked any enthusiasm.

Linc felt his stomach lunge into his chest when he saw her head suddenly tilt back and her eyes shut. "Jillian," he cried out. He rushed forward and caught her before she fell from the chair. He carried her to the sofa and laid her down. Wiping her face with the cloth, he began calling her name, trying to bring her back to consciousness.

Her eyes fluttered once, twice, and then she was looking at him blankly. "What happened?"

Linc's face was only inches from hers. "You fainted," he said softly.

"I never faint."

"You fainted, Jillian," Linc repeated softly, solely for her benefit. His gut tightened as he searched her eyes. He knew he was going to kiss her. She looked too vulnerable...too much in need of protection for him not to. Jillian needed someone who would love her and take care of her for all time. And in that moment, more than anything, Linc found he wanted to be that someone.

Her lips were soft as he gently covered her mouth with his. Just as before, she tasted so sweet and wholesome that Linc wished he could have consumed all of her.

She didn't only look vulnerable, she was vulnerable.

Fragile. That was the word he'd been searching his brain to find. To him, she was as fragile as fine-blown glass.

Opening his eyes, Linc lifted his mouth from Jillian's. Slowly, as though she was intent on savoring every moment, her eyes finally fluttered open and gazed into his.

Susceptible to her feelings, he smiled tenderly.

Faltering only momentarily, she smiled back.

"Hi," he said, making it sound as though they'd just met.

"Hi," she replied.

"Feeling better?"

She nodded slightly.

"Can you sit up?"

"I think so," she replied.

"Want to try? I'll help you."

She nodded and began to rise.

Linc slipped his arm around her shoulders and supported her. Just then, Eric and Gram entered the room.

"What happened, Mom?" Eric asked.

"Your mama fainted," Linc replied.

Gram immediately placed her hand on Jillian's forehead. "You'd better get into some dry clothes before you catch a cold—or worse, the flu." She glanced over at Linc. "You had better do the same, young man."

"Yeah," Linc replied as he stood. "I guess I should. But Jillian's injuries still need tending to."

"Let me see," Gram insisted.

Jillian held out her arms.

"Does it hurt, Mom?" Eric asked.

"Not much," Jillian replied, but the truth was, her arms were beginning to hurt her more and more. She looked up at Gram. "Do you think that you and Eric can handle the store for a while? I think I need to rest for an hour or so."

"Of course we can. Can't we, Eric?" Gram said, sounding almost offended that anyone would think she couldn't.

"Sure we can, Gram," Eric said confidently.

Linc headed for the door. "I'll go change while Jillian does the same. Then I'll come back to clean and bandage her wounds. After that, I'll go up front to help you all out in any way I can."

"That's fine," Gram stated, sounding strong and in control. She turned toward her daughter-in-law. "Now, come on, Jillian. This time I'll be the one helping you to the bathroom."

"I can help, too," Eric said.

Suddenly, Linc whirled around and walked back to Jillian. Eric and Gram automatically stepped aside. "Let's make this simple," he said, swooping down and lifting her into his arms. Jillian sucked in a deep breath, but Gram and Eric just stared at him in surprise. "Now," he said, grinning as he looked from one to the other, "which way is the bathroom?"

"This way," Eric said in a voice that sounded as though it came from a wooden puppet.

Linc marched in the direction Eric had pointed out with Jillian in his arms and Eric and Gram close at his heels. When he reached the bathroom, he carried Jillian to the tub and sat her on the edge. Gram and Eric framed the doorway.

Jillian looked flustered by all the attention. "I'll be fine," she was saying as she waved them all away. "Just go on about your business and don't worry about me. I can take care of myself."

Stepping back, Linc placed his hands on his hips. "Well, you didn't do such a great job of it earlier. That stunt you pulled could have cost you your life."

"Stunt?" Jillian repeated. "I'll have you know..." She paused in midsentence, just long enough for her gaze to change from amazement to anger. Her hands moved to her own hips. "You have some nerve. Why didn't you come down from the roof when the weather got bad like you were supposed to? Like any normal person would have?"

"I did come down."

"Then where were you?"

"Getting my motorcycle under cover from the coming rain."

An incredulous expression took hold of Jillian's features. "It certainly took you long enough. We must have waited twenty minutes for you to come inside."

"Well," Linc said, shifting his weight from one foot to the other, "I probably didn't come down from the roof right away." Then he gazed directly at her. "Hey, I'm sorry. I had no idea that you—or anyone, for that matter—would come looking for me. I'm not accustomed to having anyone concern themselves with my whereabouts. In the past, I've always taken care of myself."

"I find that hard to believe. I'm sure there was a time when your mother—"

"My mother's dead. But when she was alive, she had enough things to worry about. So I tried not to be one of them."

"And your father?"

"I never knew him," Linc answered point-blank.

Embarrassed by her own boldness, Jillian dropped her gaze to her lap. "I'm sorry," she said.

"Don't be," Linc replied. "It was his choice, not mine."

Jillian lifted her eyes and saw the cool exterior he wanted her to see. But inside, Linc Easy Rider was hurting. Big time.

He just hated to admit it, even to himself.

Eric stepped forward. "I'm really glad that Mom's okay and that you're okay, too, Linc." Then he turned quickly and hurried out of the bathroom. Without uttering a word in response, Gram simply nodded in agreement and then followed after him.

"After you've changed into something dry, get your first-aid kit. I'll be back in five minutes to help you get your wounds dressed."

Jillian glanced down at her forearms. "There's no need for that. They're not serious."

"You were bleeding," Linc said. "And that's serious. Infection could set in. And by the way, when was the last time you had a tetanus shot?"

"Tetanus? You can't be serious," Jillian said laughingly.

"That many years, huh?"

Jillian didn't know what to say. "I honestly don't know how long it's been. But there's no need—"

"There most certainly is. Years ago a friend of mine got real sick because he hurt himself and didn't bother to go to the doctor for a tetanus like he should have."

"How sick?" Jillian asked.

"Very sick," Linc answered. "He died from it."

Jillian gave a humorless laugh. "You're just trying to scare me," she said.

"No, ma'am, I'm not. So get dressed. I'm taking you to your family doctor right now."

"I don't have the money to go to the doctor for something as minor as a few scratches."

"If it were Eric who needed a tetanus, would you go?"

"Well, of course."

Linc stepped up to her, leaned close, and captured her chin, forcing her to look at him. "This is not a minor thing. You can't take a chance. I saw what happened to my friend. I will not let something like that happen to you." He released her. "Now get into some dry clothes. I'll be back before you know it. And I am taking you to the doctor, even if I have to drag you there. Do I make myself clear?"

Jillian was piqued, but she wasn't stupid. From the fiery look in his eyes, she knew he meant what he said. "Quite."

"Good," he replied. Then he spun on his heels and walked out.

Jillian was furious with his bossiness. But at the same time, she felt a sweet, delicious warmth spread deep down inside her at the thought that he cared enough about her welfare to insist she get medical attention. No one in her life thus far had ever insisted she take care of herself. Not ever.

If she didn't cooperate with his wishes, would he really *drag her* to the doctor's office like he'd said?

For some reason, she wanted to believe he would.

Chapter Eight

"Where did you put the keys to the pickup?" Linc asked, walking into the kitchen where Jillian sat. He hadn't bothered to knock first.

Lifting her head, Jillian continued dabbing lightly at her injuries with gauze she'd dampened with hydrogen peroxide from the first-aid kit. "The keys are on the wall by the refrigerator. But Old Yeller won't crank for just anyone. He's temperamental. I'll have to drive. That is, if you're still insisting that we go."

"Jillian, you *are* going to the doctor," Linc said, turning his head in her direction as he went over to get the keys. Then he added, "Come hell or high water. So stop trying to get out of it. And as for Old Yeller, I drove the truck this morning, remember?"

Jillian cut her eyes to him. "You were just lucky he cranked for you."

He tucked the key chain into his front jeans' pocket and walked back toward Jillian. "Oh . . . I wouldn't call it luck.

I happen to know a little something about vehicles. I'll get that old pickup to crank for me again, just you wait and see." Then he dropped down on one knee and swiped the medicated gauze from Jillian's fingertips. "Let me do that."

Jillian exhaled deeply. "Are you always so bossy?"

"Not always. Only when I'm dealing with someone who's every bit as *temperamental* as you claim Old Yeller to be."

She glared at him.

The corners of his mouth lifted in what Jillian considered an annoying smile. Then his gaze dropped from hers as he continued to administer the peroxide to her wounds in the same fashion as she had been doing. After he finished, he covered up her scratches with long strips of gauze that he taped in place. "There," he said. "That ought to do it until we reach a doctor's office."

Jillian looked at the bandages. "The doctor's going to think I'm an overreacting idiot when I show up in his office with these measly scratches."

"You have more than just a few measly scratches," Linc said, lifting her left arm and turning it as though he was again examining her injuries. He touched the gauze lightly in an area near her elbow. "Some of the scratches are deep, and I noticed on this arm, in particular, the skin was actually punctured right about here."

She removed her arm from his hold. "It's nothing."

"You need a tetanus injection."

"And what if the doctor says I don't need one?" Jillian asked. "What then?"

"Then we'll come home and you'll be able to say *I told you so.* But if I'm right and you do need an injection . . ."

"I'm sure you won't let me forget it any time soon. Right?"

His grin was sarcastic, but at the same time, downright sexy.

Not that she cared if his smile was sexy or not. It was simply an observation.

"Right," he said.

Suddenly Linc's face went blank and he stood erect. "Actually, I won't be around here long enough for it to matter one way or the other, now will I?"

"Correct," Jillian quickly agreed. She certainly didn't want him thinking that she had changed her mind about him. Because she hadn't. His job as her handyman was temporary. And that was that.

Besides, she reminded herself, his state of employment was as much to his liking as it was to hers.

When she looked up and found him gazing at her with those blue eyes of his like he was doing now, it was enough to drive her mad. This time, though, she had the strangest feeling. They reminded her of another time, or maybe another person, but the moment was so fleeting, she didn't have the opportunity to jar loose the forgotten memory. Maybe it would come to her later.

Taking a deep, steadying breath, Jillian placed her hand over her pounding heart and wondered if the hydrogen peroxide she'd applied to her wounds had gotten into her bloodstream and was now causing her heart to jackhammer around in her chest. Good Lord, at the moment it was pounding away at the base of her throat. She wasn't a nurse or anything, and she certainly wasn't qualified to make any kind of diagnosis, but wouldn't something like that make a person's heart act a little crazy? Pound a little faster?

Well, one thing was for sure. There was no way she was going to admit that her erratic heartbeat had anything to do with Linc Rider or his cocky smile. Nor did it have anything to do with the way he was now gazing at her with those lethal blue eyes of his.

"Let's go," he said curtly.

Reacting to the gruffness in his voice, Jillian shot up from her chair. "What about Eric and Gram? Shouldn't we say something to them before leaving?" she asked.

"I've already told them that I'm taking you to the doctor," Linc replied, opening the back door and motioning for her to walk out before him. "So quit looking for excuses to delay us. They simply won't work."

Resigning herself to the fact that she *was* going to a doctor's office—as Linc had so politely put it, come hell or high water—Jillian marched briskly through the door and down the back steps. Linc caught up with her and they walked side by side until they reached the garage. Then Linc went ahead of her to open the passenger door on her truck and waited to help her climb inside. Afterward, he hurried around the back of the pickup and got in behind the steering wheel.

Confident, he stuck the key in the ignition and clicked it on. The engine turned over a couple of times, then it sputtered and coughed, before dying out completely. Linc pumped the accelerator several times and then tried again. This time the truck sputtered three times and coughed twice before finally dying out.

Linc cursed under his breath. Jillian cleared her throat in an I-told-you-so fashion that only fueled his growing irritation. He pounded hard on the accelerator and then pushed it down to the floorboard. He clicked on the ignition and once more Old Yeller started up, sputtering and coughing, just as before. He gave the engine gas, but it didn't seem to have any effect. And then, just when it appeared that the engine was smothering itself out, the ornery old pickup coughed out a tail of black smoke and roared back to life. An immediate grin sprang to Linc's face.

"See," he said confidently, "I told you this old pickup had met his match."

As soon as he said it, the truck died out again. His face crumbled into a look of disbelief.

"Uh-huh," Jillian replied. "Looks like Old Yeller's met his match, all right."

Linc leaned back in the brown vinyl seat and took a deep breath. He didn't doubt for a minute that he could get this damned old pickup going. But after the way he'd just bragged to Jillian, he hated having to get out of the vehicle and look under its hood. Besides, he'd probably end up getting himself all dirty. Then who would drive Jillian to get the medical attention she needed? Certainly, she wouldn't.

Suddenly he sat up, grabbed hold of the steering wheel with one hand and place the other on the ignition. "Come on, Yeller," he said under his breath, "it's you and me against the odds." Then to Jillian, he said, "Brace yourself, baby. 'Cause this is it."

Unconsciously, Linc held his breath. "Come on. This is your last chance," he said, as though Old Yeller would understand his warning. The engine turned over twice before it suddenly sputtered and coughed to life. Once more, Linc fed gasoline to the engine. But it wasn't until after a few touch-and-go moments where it looked as though Old Yeller would die out again that its engine was finally able to blow out all the cobwebs that had been choking it and start to run smoothly.

Linc's face beamed with pride. "Atta boy," he said to Old Yeller, patting the dashboard first, then throwing the truck into reverse. He looked at Jillian. "See? I told you I could get Old Yeller cranked." He held up one hand. "It's all in the touch, baby. All in the touch."

His grin was so contagious, Jillian had to smile, too. "What do you mean?" she asked.

His grin slipped up one side of his face, causing Jillian's stomach to jump into her throat.

"Well," he drawled, his Southern accent suddenly becoming very prevalent, "I learned a long time ago that a *temperamental* vehicle is a lot like a *temperamental* woman." He took a moment to gun the accelerator. "Listen to that," he said to Jillian in a smooth voice. "To make an engine purr like that, you've got to have the right touch. The same applies to a woman."

"That's ridiculous. Old Yeller didn't respond to some special touch of yours. The engine cranked—period," Jillian said.

"Well, that ain't exactly the way I see it," he said, now exaggerating his accent, as well as his way of speaking.

"So what's your point?" Jillian asked, trying to act as though she were getting bored with his little game, when in reality she was fighting back the rush of emotion he always seemed so easily to cause in her.

"My point is that *two out of two* ain't bad. In fact, that's a pretty darn good score. Wouldn't you agree?" His grin was now beyond being cocky. It was downright sinful.

Jillian deliberately shrugged as though she hadn't a care in the world. "I have no idea what you're talking about."

"You and Old Yeller. Both of you are temperamental. And both of you responded to the right touch."

That was the *second time* he'd referred to her as being temperamental. "That's crazy," she retorted. "I *am not* temperamental. And besides, even if I were, you know good and well that you've never touched me in any way."

"You *are* temperamental," he said point-blank. "And I *have* touched you. Or have you forgotten the time we kissed and—"

Jillian sat up. "Are you going to take me to the doctor or not?" she asked in a curt tone of voice. "Because if you're not, I have work to do." Popping open the passenger door, she glanced at Linc in a way that suggested she was ready to jump out of the truck and get on with her chores. All he had to do was say the word.

"Get back in here and shut the damned door," Linc growled, gunning the motor loudly.

Reacting to the authority in his voice, Jillian slammed the door and crossed her arms at her waist, causing her scratches to ache even more. But she was too angry with Linc to give him the satisfaction of knowing her injuries were beginning to throb. *Temperamental?* Uh-uh. No, indeed. *Not her.*

As soon as she shut the door, Linc gunned the motor and Old Yeller shot out of the garage. He braked to a sudden halt just before reaching the end of the driveway. Jillian grabbed hold of the dash to steady herself. "My God, can you even drive this thing?"

Linc didn't bother to answer her question. "Which way?" he demanded.

"That way," Jillian replied, pointing to her left. "My doctor's practice is in Bunkie. That's about fifteen miles from here."

"I know how to get there," he said sorely. "From Baton Rouge I came up Highway 71."

"Good," she replied in the same tone of voice. "Then we shouldn't have to speak to each other again until we get to the city limits."

"How rewarding to know," he answered dryly, grinding the transmission gears as he shifted into first and Old Yeller jerked forward.

Jillian was given a tetanus injection after her doctor checked her records and found she hadn't had one since she'd stepped on a nail back in high school. Then she had to listen to his five-minute lecture on the importance of keeping one's immunizations updated—even as an adult.

Linc's gloating over the diagnosis was obvious, even to the attractive nurse who made a comment about it while she gave Jillian the tetanus injection. Actually, he looked so puffed up with the desire to tell her *I told you so* that Jillian began to think he resembled a blowfish. A big, twenty-pound blowfish. Hopefully, either she or someone else would come along and find a way to scale him back down to size. Otherwise, she'd be at his mercy until he got tired of goading her.

But, if she was going to be the sort of person who tried to be honest with herself—at least from time to time—then she had to admit that the thought of her being at his mercy didn't seem half-bad at the moment. Which should've warned her right off that her common sense had gone into hiding somewhere. But somehow, she missed the clue completely. Instead, she lifted her eyes to his and allowed herself the temporary luxury of wondering what it would be like to make love with a man like Linc Rider.

And then suddenly she got a clear image of the two of them in bed . . . naked . . . and hot . . . and . . .

Good grief, but it's getting warm in this place, Jillian thought, picking up a magazine from a nearby table and fanning herself.

Linc cleared his throat. "You look flushed, Jillian. Are you feeling okay?" he asked, sliding off the metal stool he'd sat on since entering the examination room with her. He placed the backs of his fingers lightly against her forehead.

Jillian's cheeks flamed even more with color. "Uh, yes...I feel fine. It's warm in here, that's all."

"Maybe you're having an allergic reaction to the tetanus shot. The nurse did say we had to wait twenty minutes before leaving."

"No, that's not it," she said, pushing his hand away. "I'm telling you I feel fine."

"You probably wouldn't tell me the truth anyway."

Irritated that she had been lost in ridiculous thoughts of the two of them in bed together while he had sat there and pegged her so accurately, at least where her attitude on being ill was concerned, she snapped back, "Then why bother to ask me, if you don't believe anything I say?"

Suddenly the door to the examination room opened and the nurse who'd tended to her earlier stepped inside. "You can go now, hon. But if any problem should arise, call us right away." She turned to leave, but then halted and whirled back around to Jillian with a glowing smile on her face. "Oh...and next time, be more careful when you climb up a ladder," she said.

Startled that the woman should know any of the details of her accident, Jillian gaped. "How did you know—"

The nurse nodded her head toward Linc. "He told me," she said, giving Linc a full-blown smile. When she glanced back at Jillian and saw the bewildered look on her patient's face, the woman's smile faded somewhat. "While we was waiting here for you to return from down the hall with your specimen."

Oh, good grief, Jillian thought. The two of them had been standing around, flirting with each other while she was in the rest room. *How charming.*

The nurse looked at Linc and the two of them smiled as though they shared some intimate little secret. Pure jealousy, disguised as adrenaline, gushed through Jillian's veins.

The nurse shook her head in mock disbelief. "That was quite a story, hearing how Linc found you dangling from the rooftop in the middle of that downpour we had earlier.

"My...my..." she continued almost breathlessly. "And then for him to get there just in time to save you from plunging to your death.... How romantic."

Plunging to her death? *How romantic, indeed.* And the woman had the nerve to call Linc by his first name, no less. *How quaint.*

"Can I go now?" Jillian asked dryly. "I've got things to do back home."

"Sure," the nurse said. "Just don't hesitate to call us if you need anything."

"Thanks. We won't," Linc replied, placing his hand at the small of Jillian's back. She slipped off the examination table. "Are you sure that you feel okay?" he continued, lifting her chin until she was forced to gaze into his eyes.

How could she feel okay when she was drowning in a sea of intense, blue eyes? "Don't worry about me," she sputtered. "I—I'm fine. Really I am."

Ignoring the nurse who was watching from a few feet away, he leaned forward and lightly kissed her on the lips. "Somebody needs to worry about you, Jillian. Because you sure as hell don't."

He'd kissed her, for heaven's sake. Right on the mouth. Right in front of the nurse *he* had been flirting with. As if it was something he did all the time. As if it was something he knew she wanted him to do.

But she didn't.

Did.

Not.

Flustered, Jillian lowered her gaze to the middle of Linc's chest. Then she looked over and saw that the nurse was now wearing less of a smile than earlier. Actually, it kind of wobbled at the corners.

Linc and Jillian left the doctor's office and started the drive back home. Obviously, somewhere along the way to her doctor, Linc and Old Yeller had become the best of friends. Because now when Linc turned on the ignition, Old Yeller cranked. Without fail.

Heading out of town, Linc pulled over at a fast-food restaurant and bought them each a milk shake. He wanted strawberry. Jillian preferred chocolate. But now, only a few miles farther down the road, she was already threatening to pour her chocolate shake, along with his strawberry one, down the front of his shirt if he didn't learn to drive more cautiously.

Heck. He thought he was a damned good driver. No one had ever complained to him before, not that he could recall, anyway. Of course, he didn't remember the last time he'd actually driven anything other than his motorcycle. Still, she didn't have to get all bent out of shape just because he didn't *always* stay within the constraints of the two white lines on either side of him. Good grief, he was driving down a highway in the middle of nowhere and there wasn't another vehicle in sight. He knew what he was doing.

Women. Nag. Nag. Nag.

So why was it that he was enjoying himself so much? Why was it that he felt so good inside, almost peaceful, at the thought that he and Jillian were heading back home—together—like a happily married couple? And that Eric—their son—would be there, waiting for them? Because if he knew anything at all, he knew this wasn't his life, nor was it meant to be. This moment wasn't any more his than was this old pickup he was driving. Nothing surrounding him was for real. *He* wasn't for real.

Suddenly, just as quickly as they had come, the good feelings he'd had inside just a few moments ago were gone. Just like that. Like a snap of the fingers. One good dose of pure reality and—bam—they were off and running for cover, leaving him with the same low-down feelings he'd experienced as a kid. Back then, nothing good had ever lasted for very long, either. Apparently, for him, nothing ever would.

Jillian watched the dramatic play of conflicting emotions on Linc's face. From thoughtfulness...to contentment...to blankness...to sadness. She'd seen them all come and go within moments of each other. Except for the sadness. It still lingered.

What was he thinking about? she wondered. She wanted to say something to him...anything, really, that would comfort him, make him feel better—quickly. She hated seeing him like this. Whatever it was that was bothering him, he certainly didn't deserve the trouncing. Not today, anyway. Because today he'd saved her life and that made him a kind of hero. *Her* hero, to be exact. And if she could bring herself to swallow her pride long enough to thank him properly, she knew she'd feel a whole lot better about herself.

"Pull over," she said quietly.

"What?" he exclaimed, glancing over at her.

She smiled sweetly at him. "I said, *pull over.*"

He looked at her as though she were crazy. "Why? I'm staying between the lines now, just like you wanted."

"Just pull over—please," she added with emphasis.

Linc peered at her for a couple of seconds. Then he looked straight ahead, and then finally back at her, a disbelieving expression on his face. Shaking his head, he pulled the pickup to the shoulder of the road and braked it to a stop. "Okay. What's wrong, now, Little Miss Muffet?"

"Kill the motor," she ordered calmly.

Staring at the road ahead, he hesitated for a moment, but eventually did as she asked.

"Thank you."

"You're welcome," he replied without glancing at her. He sat back, placed his arm along the back of the seat, allowing his hand to come to a rest right behind her left shoulder, and sighed deeply. "Now, would you kindly tell me what this is all about?"

"You," she stated honestly.

Swinging his head around to face her, he narrowed his gaze. Finally he grinned and then lifted up his hands in a frustrated manner. "What in the hell did I do wrong now?"

"Nothing," Jillian replied sweetly, smiling at him. "I just wanted to say that I owe you my gratitude."

Her words deflated Linc. He sank back in the seat and stared at her.

Good grief! Did she have any idea what she did to him when she smiled at him like that? His self-control had just shattered to pieces like glass, that was what. And because his composure was now in bits and pieces at his feet, his gut was rocking and rolling around in him as though it were some kind of crazed rock singer. What in the hell was she trying to do to him, anyway? But worse, why was he allowing her to get to him in the first place?

Because you're getting as soft as a mama's boy, that's why, he told himself. He didn't know how, or even when it had happened, but somewhere between finding his son and getting to know Jillian, he had lost the emotional shell he once had. The anger he'd had from growing up on the streets seemed almost foreign to him now. Almost as though it had been someone else's life.

He glanced at Jillian and saw that she was still smiling at him. Grinning back at her, he said, "I know what it is. You're having a reaction to the tetanus shot, right?"

She shook her head. "Wrong."

Finishing his milk shake, Linc crushed the paper cup in one hand and placed it on the floorboard near his door. But when Jillian lifted hers to take a sip, he suddenly swiped it from her hand and brought it near the front windshield as though to examine its contents in the bright sunlight. "By golly, somebody must've spiked your milk shake," he said seriously.

For Jillian, the surprise of having her drink snatched away took a moment to wear off. But when it did, she just as quickly stole it back from him. "Stop being ridiculous."

"I mean it," Linc said.

But by now Jillian could see another grin tickling at the corners of his mouth.

"Something's got to be wrong with you," Linc vowed solemnly. "You've never been this nice. At least, not to me. But I kind of like it. Maybe you could make this a habit. What do you say?"

"I thought you weren't going to be around here for long enough for anything to become a habit. Didn't you say that?"

Linc's grin evaporated and he glanced off into the distance. "Yeah, I probably once said something to that effect."

"Did you mean it?" Jillian asked, finding herself holding her breath, waiting for his answer. Good grief, what was she hoping he'd say?

"Uh, yeah," Linc said in a noncommittal tone of voice. He continued staring straight ahead. "I meant it. Why else would I have said it?"

Jillian felt her heart slowly, but surely, go slip-sliding away. "No reason that I can think of." She took a deep breath and then stared out the window on the passenger side. "Well, I still owe you my thanks. So if I can help you in any way—ever—just let me know."

"Yeah...sure," he said, cranking up Old Yeller. He shifted into gear, checked to see if there was any oncoming traffic and drove off when he saw it was clear.

They rode in silence for a short time. Finally, Linc broke the heavy barrier. "I bet you've always lived right here in Pine Creek."

"Yes, I have."

"Have you ever dreamed of moving someplace else?"

Jillian smirked. "I've dreamed of moving just about anyplace else—at least twice."

"Then why haven't you?"

Jillian took a deep breath and then shrugged. "I don't know. Obligations, I guess. Fate. Who knows? Besides, running never seems to be the right answer. Not for me, anyway."

"Duty-bound at age thirty-four," he stated.

Jillian drew her eyebrows together. "How do you know my age?"

Linc's cheerful mood came to a fast halt. "Uh, you told me, I guess."

"I don't remember telling you that."

Looking directly into her eyes, Linc shrugged. "I can't say that I remember the exact conversation, either. But how else would I know it?"

For once Jillian tried gazing into his eyes, hoping to gain a better understanding of the mystery man she'd hired. But what she received as her reward was only a slight smile from him before he deviated his hooded eyes back to the road ahead. Which was a pretty sneaky move on his part, Jillian thought, even if he was the one doing the driving. Once again, she gazed out the passenger window.

"Did I ever tell you that my mother died before her thirty-second birthday?" Linc asked.

Jillian's eyes widened in surprise. But when she spoke, her voice was compassionate. "She was so young. It must've been terrible for you."

"She just gave up on life. I realize that now. But at the time...I didn't understand what was happening."

"Why did she give up? Was she terminally ill?"

Linc groaned. "Yeah, you could say that. I guess her life-style did become a kind of cancer for her. It damned sure ate up her insides. Toward the end she didn't care about anything anymore."

"Not even you?"

"Jillian, my mother lost her chance for a decent life when she was only sixteen years old. Pregnant and alone, she took to the streets to earn money to support herself and her baby—me. Do you have any idea what that kind of life does to a woman?" Linc asked. Then immediately he replied, "Of course you don't."

"I'm not judging her," Jillian cut in. "So you don't have to explain anything to me if you don't want to."

"Maybe I want to," he replied.

"Then if that's what you feel you need to do, I'm willing to listen," Jillian said.

Gazing at him from where she sat, Jillian thought there were tears in his eyes. Her heart constricted. She knew he was hurting. Linc Rider wasn't a man who cried easily. Then he was looking back at her and her heart took a fluttering leap into her throat. "How about you, sweet Jillian? Are you gonna let your chance at life pass you by, like my mother did?"

She blinked. "Uh—of c-course not," she stammered.

"Then what are you waiting for? Or rather, *who* are you waiting for?"

"Nothing...no one," Jillian replied. "I don't know what you mean."

"I think you do," Linc insisted.

"I don't take unnecessary chances, if that's what you're talking about."

"Like the chance of meeting someone and falling in love?"

Jillian shook her head. "That's not likely to happen."

"Why? Aren't you hoping to remarry someday?"

"Hoping to . . . ?" she repeated. Then slowly shaking her head, she said, "No, I can't say as I'm hoping to remarry someday."

"What if Mr. Perfect suddenly shows up in your life?"

Maybe he has, Jillian found herself mentally replying.

Then her breath locked in her throat.

"I don't need a Mr. Perfect."

Linc glanced at her in a way that suggested he agreed with her. Wholeheartedly. Her stomach sank to the floorboard. And in that brief second, Jillian knew without a doubt that if she were given a choice of whom she wanted to spend the remainder of her life with, *he* would have been her pick in that moment. Hands down.

But only in that moment. Which had quickly passed, thank God. Now she was thinking clearly again.

Suddenly, Linc slowed Old Yeller and turned the pickup down a narrow dirt road to their right that cut through a field of sugarcane. The road led to a clump of tall trees.

"Where are you going?"

"You'll see."

"Linc..." Jillian began. "What on earth...? Don't you realize it's almost sunset?"

"I know. Just trust me on this, will you?"

"But—"

"Please..."

Jillian leaned back in her seat. Did she really have a choice? "Only if you promise to get us home before dark. I have chores to do."

They quickly arrived at the end of the dirt road and Jillian saw that the clump of trees she had seen from the main highway was in fact a small grove of rather large pecan trees. Linc braked Old Yeller to a halt under the shade of the tallest one. Then he killed the engine and turned in his seat so that he faced her.

"Now..." he stated.

A sense of apprehension tingled along Jillian's spine. She shivered.

"Cold?"

"No."

"Scared?"

"Uh-uh," she replied.

"Have you ever been parking with a guy before?" he said, casually slipping a toothpick from his T-shirt pocket and placing it in one corner of his mouth. After biting down on it, he leaned back and began watching her.

"I don't have time for these games, Linc. I really do need to get home," Jillian stated, ignoring the way he could make her feel as though she were going to smother to death right then and there if he didn't kiss her on the mouth. For goodness' sake, she didn't even *want* him to kiss her.

You do.

Not.

"You'll get home all in good time, sweet Jillian. All in good time."

His teasing, "easy come, easy go" tone of voice caused a chill to slither down her spine. It wasn't that she was afraid of him—exactly. It was just that she always felt as though she were being consumed alive. As though his blue eyes could see beyond her skin. She didn't know how he did it, but Linc Rider had a way of tapping right into her very soul. And that made him extremely dangerous to her. "What is it you want from me, Linc?"

Working his jaw as he peered at her, Linc shoved back his dark hair with long, skillful fingers. Then, narrowing his eyes, he looked away into the distance at the setting sun. "I honestly don't know," he said.

"But you do want something, don't you?"

"Maybe. Maybe not."

"Is it money?"

"What?" he exclaimed.

"Is it money you're after? Because if it is, you're going to be very disappointed. I don't have any," Jillian said.

Linc gaped at her. "For heaven's sake, Jillian, if it were money I was after, I wouldn't be in this two-bit town, hustling a widow who's working herself to the bone trying to make ends meet, now would I?"

He had a point, Jillian thought. "So what *are* you after, then?"

Linc glanced back toward the setting sun. In that moment, it would have been so easy for him to answer that question for her. Eric. You. Love. Home. Family. Forgiveness. *A new start.*

But he knew in his heart it was too late for all that. It had always been too late. Like his mother, he had lost his one chance at happiness a long time ago.

And now he was scared. Scared of having to let go of the one person he loved more than life itself.

His son.

And yes, dammit. He'd have to let go of Jillian, too.

And that made him sad.

Chapter Nine

Linc chose to ignore his own warning signals where Jillian was concerned. Instead, he slipped his hand across her shoulders and gently eased her toward him. Pausing momentarily when their faces were mere inches apart, his gaze dropped to her mouth.

"What is it?" she asked breathlessly.

He lifted his eyes. "This is your last chance, Jillian."

Jillian's breath caught in her throat. Not even for a million dollars could she have found the strength to stop him from doing what she knew he intended. Because in that moment, she wanted him more than anything.

Then he was kissing her gently, almost shyly, before slowly withdrawing just enough to say, "Open your mouth, Jillian. I want to taste your sweetness." Next, he ran his moist, hot tongue across her lips. "Come on. Just relax, baby."

A sudden, pulsating heat rushed out from every sleeping cell in Jillian's body and, like a wound-up toy soldier, marched its way to her lower abdomen. She leaned closer to him and her mouth opened involuntarily.

Linc smiled. "Atta girl," he coaxed. And then he took her lips with his and leisurely plundered her inner mouth with a sensuous, erotic rhythm that drove them both wild with desire for what seemed like endless moments.

Then Jillian was trying to pull away and Linc found himself wrestling with the thought of never letting her go. At least, not just yet. And that was when he knew without a doubt that he would never, ever, have enough of this woman. Unconsciously, he lifted his hands and cupped the sides of her face, holding her head firmly in place. In his unbridled need to taste her sweetness to the very end, he didn't realize the forcefulness of his actions.

But Jillian did, and she had to fight the swell of panic that suddenly rose in her throat. After all, she was alone in a deserted place with a man she barely knew.

"Linc...no...stop...let go of me," she cried out, her hands pulling at his to release her.

Realizing that his actions were totally out of character for him—he'd never forced a woman to do anything against her will—Linc immediately dropped his hands from her face and sat back against the seat, taking deep breaths and trying to make some sense of the past few crazy moments in his life. Bewildered, he used both of his hands to comb back his hair. Then he dragged his fingertips down his face in an attempt to make certain that what he thought had happened wasn't, in reality, just a bad dream.

It wasn't.

Groping for air, Jillian sat back in her seat, only she slid as far away from him as the small cab would allow her. Her lips were still burning from his kisses. But that was the only part of her body that he was ever going to hurt again. At least, if she had anything to say about it. And that included her heart. "So this is what you thought you'd get from me," she said, her voice shaking with anger. Her trust in him—in herself—was shattered.

"Ah, hell . . ." he said, leaning his forehead against the steering wheel in disgust. Then he tilted his head back and sighed deeply. "Would it make any difference if I said no?"

Without giving him the benefit of an answer, Jillian clasped her hands together in her lap and looked out the window to her right.

In a sudden hurry to be someplace else—or rather, anyplace else—he cranked up Old Yeller. "I thought not," he growled under his breath as he turned the pickup around and headed back toward the main road. Still fuming on the inside, he didn't bother to slow his speed when he reached the highway and saw it was vacant. And when the worn tires on Old Yeller hit the raised edge of the asphalt pavement, the shock of it sent the old pickup—and its occupants—bouncing onto the highway. The engine choked and Linc shifted down to second gear. The truck backfired twice and then shot forward down the road. The entire time Jillian hung on to the dash to keep from being thrown from her seat. But this time, she didn't mutter a sound about his driving.

Upon returning home, they found Gram and Eric waiting on them. After Jillian explained to Gram that her condition wasn't serious, the old woman turned to Linc and Eric and ordered them to wash up for supper. Eric, hearing the news for the first time that they were having tuna salad sandwiches, made a disgusted face and complained that he didn't like tuna fish. But when his grandmother said she didn't own a cafeteria and it was eat that or nothing at all, he fixed himself two sandwiches and then grabbed a handful of barbecued-flavored potato chips.

Linc surprised everyone by first fixing Jillian a plate of food and then doing the same for Gram before filling his own plate with sandwiches and chips. Sitting in a chair next to Eric, he waited in silence while the others said grace. When they were done, Jillian stood and began pouring milk into everyone's glasses. Linc reached over and took the plastic container from her. "I don't think you ought to be using your arms so much," he said. He finished filling the glasses.

Jillian watched him intently. As of yet, the two of them hadn't resolved their differences from earlier. Actually, Jillian sincerely thought it was for the best if they didn't. She had hoped that from now on, he'd mind his own business, and she'd mind hers.

Jillian looked at Gram. "Were you very busy while we were gone?"

"There was the usual afternoon rush. But that's all," Gram replied. "Oh . . . there was something . . ."

"What was it?" Jillian asked.

"The telephone rang on two separate occasions, I believe," Gram said, sounding unsure of herself. "Or maybe it was three times. Eric, do you remember?"

"I think it was three times, Gram. I answered it the first time. Then you answered it twice after that," Eric said.

"That's right," Gram replied. "Now I remember."

"Well," Jillian said, "who was it?"

"We don't know," Eric replied. "The one time I answered, no one was on the line."

Gram was nodding her head. "That's right. And when I answered the first time, there was a long pause before a woman asked who was speaking. I identified myself and then she hung up. The next time I answered, the caller hung up the moment I said hello. I think all three calls were made by the same person."

"Me, too," Eric chimed in.

"Probably just a wrong number," Jillian said. "We get them every once in a while."

Gram looked over at Linc with an inquisitive expression on her face. "That's what it sounds like to me," Linc answered.

Gram shook her head in disbelief. "I tell you, people of today don't have the manners of my generation."

Eric's eyes widened. "Gram, were there really telephones when you were little?"

"Of course there were," she answered gruffly. "Not nearly as many as today, though."

Eric chomped down on his sandwich, then drank several swallows of milk to wash it down before using his hand instead of his paper napkin to wipe the corners of his mouth. He was preparing to take another bite when he stopped and looked up at his mother. "Mom, you remember the all-star tournament I told you about? Well, my first game is tomorrow. You didn't forget, did you?"

Jillian was startled by the news, but pretended otherwise. "No, I didn't forget."

"You will come, won't you?" he asked.

For a moment, Jillian gazed down at her plate. Then, squaring her shoulders, she glanced up and smiled at her son. "What time does the game start, Eric?"

"Two o'clock."

"I'm going to try real hard to be there. But because of the store, you know I can't make any promises."

"I know," Eric replied, a hint of disappointment in his voice. "But please try, Mom."

Jillian's heart constricted. She couldn't let down her son again. Somehow she was going to find a way to go to that game. Even if it meant she would have to close down business for a couple of hours.

Then Eric turned and gazed at the man seated beside him. "Will you come, Linc?"

Hesitating, Linc quickly cut his eyes to Jillian and saw her troubled expression. God, but he was beginning to hate seeing her upset. Which could only mean one thing. He was heading for big trouble. "Yeah, kid, I'll be there."

Eric grinned at him and then went back to eating the food that still remained on his plate.

Linc, however, suddenly realized that his appetite had vanished. And heaven help him, he knew why.

Something had drastically changed since his arrival in Pine Creek just two days ago.

Something about *him* had drastically changed.

And that was his problem wrapped up in a nutshell, he told himself. Like a fool, he'd gone and lost his sharp edge, his sense of feeling damned near invincible. For years it had been his only weapon. But now the hard, fast rule of survival that he'd learned as a kid and, when necessary, had applied all his life, simply wasn't working anymore.

As a result, his plans—his whole future—was now in jeopardy.

He'd lost his edge, all right. He'd crossed over the fine line that divided what he really wanted in life and what he really felt he deserved. And now there was no going back to safer ground. No more fooling himself. He was standing face-to-face with reality. And the truth about himself and the lies he'd told to everyone had become ghostlike, haunting him mercilessly, day in and day out.

Kidding himself was impossible. He knew he had been willing to destroy Jillian to have his son. He wasn't worthy of her trust. Certainly, he wasn't worthy of her love.

Where Eric was concerned, he simply didn't deserve his son. Period. Trixie, for once in her life, had used her head and had done the right thing when she'd given up their baby for adoption. And lucky for Eric, he'd gotten Jillian for a mother.

Linc took a deep breath. So now he knew what he had to do.

A bittersweet smile touched at the corners of Linc's mouth, but in the end it failed to overcome a more dominant emotion and he frowned instead.

There was only one solution, and he knew it. Maybe, deep down inside, he'd always known it. Eric was only eleven years old. Far too young, Linc now realized, to have his world shaken apart by someone who didn't even know he'd existed six months ago. Not even by someone who felt he had every right. Because the timing wasn't right. As much as Linc wanted his son and as unfair as the whole situation seemed to him, until Eric was older and had a better understanding of life, Linc knew he was going to have to walk away from his son without telling the boy who he really was.

And that was facing reality.

And in doing so, he'd be walking away from the woman he had come to love.

He'd made a royal mess of things.

Now that was facing a double dose of reality. But whoever said life was fair?

Still, as sad as he felt inside, knowing he'd come to a decision—a right decision—gave him a sense of relief.

So now, if he was to carry out that decision, he knew what he had to do. And the sooner he walked away from here, the better for all concerned.

Suddenly he was jarred from his thoughts when he felt Eric nudging him in the side with his elbow. "Wanna watch TV with me for a while?" he asked.

"Ah...yeah, sure," Linc replied, glancing in Jillian's direction. "Give me a minute, okay?"

Eric excused himself from the table, carried his dirty plate and utensils to the sink and then settled down on the floor in front of the television. Gram and Jillian rose at the same time and began clearing away the table. Linc joined them. A moment later he noticed when Gram whispered something to Jillian.

Jillian listened and then said, "Maybe so. I'll have to think about it."

Gram nodded and then announced out loud for everyone to hear that she was retiring to bed.

Linc helped Jillian in the kitchen until they were finished washing and drying all the supper dishes. Their conversation consisted strictly of the task they were doing. Finally, however, Linc looked at Jillian as they stood at the kitchen sink. "I have something I need to talk to you about."

Jillian looked up at him, her eyes widening. "Oh?"

Linc's stomach churned. "Yeah, well, I'd prefer if we could wait until sometime later tonight. I was going to watch TV with Eric for a while. Then I've got someplace I need to go, but I'll be back later. I guess what I'm asking is, would you mind waiting up for me?"

Disturbed by the seriousness in his tone of voice, Jillian studied his face. She glanced down and saw his hand resting on the counter next to hers. For a fleeting moment, she'd had the craziest notion to place her hand on top of his, but, thank goodness, she reconsidered the move before making a fool of herself.

Furthermore, she needed to mind her own business. Just like he needed to mind his. How many times was she going to have to remind herself of that?

Clearing her throat, Jillian glanced up. "I'll wait up."

Linc nodded. "Good."

Jillian turned and headed down the hall. When she reached the bathroom, she stopped before entering and spun around to face him. "You've won yourself a new friend. Because of your gallant efforts to save me, Gram now thinks that you are completely trustworthy and should be allowed to sleep inside on the sofa at night. She says that you'd probably be grateful for the use of our shower, too."

A kind of sad, lopsided grin lifted one corner of his mouth. "I may have won Gram's trust, but I've lost yours, right?"

Jillian hesitated in answering him.

"Never mind," Linc said. "It's not important anyway."

He started to pivot around, but stopped himself midway through. "Oh, by the way, I'll probably be history by tomorrow afternoon."

"What?" Jillian asked, a sense of dread suddenly clouding around her.

Deep down inside, Linc had hoped his words would get a reaction from her and he was pleased to see they had. For a moment, it soothed his hurting ego. "I have reason to believe that my friend Hal is home."

"Oh," Jillian replied, wondering why his news didn't fill her with joy like it should have. Wasn't this what she had wanted all along?

Trembling, Jillian turned to enter the bathroom. Linc stood where he was and watched. After stepping through the entrance, she turned around and her eyes met his. For the next few seconds, they stared long and hard at each other until Jillian finally shut the door, separating them. Feeling breathless, she leaned her back against the frame and closed her eyes as tears sprang forth.

Linc continued to stare down the hall until he felt he had gathered his mangled feelings. He had placed everything on the line with that last statement about his leaving by tomorrow. Damn, what had he expected? For her to beg him to stay? Well, he could forget it. Jillian Fontenot was more than glad to know he'd soon be gone. His being here was a threat to her humdrum way of life—not that she'd ever admit that to herself.

Frustrated with himself—with Jillian, with life—Linc pivoted on his heels, intent on walking out. But when he saw his son sitting alone on the floor, watching TV, his knees almost buckled beneath him. He dropped into a chair just behind Eric and stretched out his legs.

"What are you watching, kid?"

Eric turned and smiled. "Baseball." He whirled back around to face the scene when the announcer's voice got excited. "Oh, boy, another homer," he exclaimed.

Linc smiled, but the gesture didn't quite make it to his eyes. Nor did it help the sick feeling he had inside.

Boys and baseball.

His boy and baseball.

Damn, he was going to miss some of the best times in Eric's life.

And for one fleeting moment, Linc regretted the decision he had made. But then he inhaled and exhaled deeply, using the time to strengthen his resolve. Because, to some degree, he knew he would always have regrets. Fair play, it seemed, came only at a heavy price.

By ten o'clock Eric was in bed and asleep. Jillian sat in a chair, watching the late-night news, waiting for Linc to return so they could have their little "talk." She was ready for him—ready to meet him head-on—and, every few minutes, glanced anxiously at the clock on the wall above the television. A commercial advertising a new health-conscious cereal had just started when she heard the roar of a motorcycle—his motorcycle, she was almost sure of it—that signaled he was back. Her heart began to pound, ignoring the fact that she had told herself he no longer affected her.

Within seconds, she heard his movements as he rolled his bike into the yard and parked it alongside the outdoor kitchen. She heard his rapid steps approaching the back porch. Then he was knocking lightly on the door.

Shaking with anticipation, Jillian stood, checking to make certain her pink cotton robe was still closed properly. Licking her lips, she smoothed back her hair from her face.

Then she walked cautiously toward the sound, peeled back the tan curtain to make sure it was Linc, and then opened up when she saw him.

"Come in," she said, stepping aside to allow him enough space to enter. By no means did she want the two of them touching. Her feelings were already topsy-turvy. His long strides took him to the center of the room, where he stopped and faced her.

Jillian smiled bitterly to herself. God, but she'd been a fool to think she could play along with Linc Rider's tantalizing little game of seduction without getting burned. He was such a pro at it, she'd never stood a chance. In less than two days, he'd managed to turn her entire world upside down. Nothing felt the same anymore. Nothing *was* the same anymore. And what scared her most was the fear that it might never be again. But the only hope of that ever happening, however slight, was to get him out of her life. Out of Eric's life. Out of Pine Creek—period.

She could see it all so clearly now. The manipulation... the way he'd worked himself into their souls. And just knowing that he was capable of walking away from her— from Eric—without a backward glance only proved what kind of a temporary man he really was. She'd had him pegged right all along. Underneath all the smiles and kisses, Linc Rider was the total opposite of the kind of man she could ever admire. Simply put, he lacked strength of character.

But her thoughts—and even her pain—wasn't what worried her the most about Linc's leaving. There were times when being a hardy woman did have its advantages. It was Eric's reaction that concerned her. He adored Linc and thought they were friends. He was going to be devastated when he heard the news.

"Sit down," Jillian said, motioning for Linc to take a seat.

"That's all right. This won't take long."

"All right," Jillian replied. "What is it you want to tell me?"

Shifting his weight to his left leg, Linc mentally prepared himself for the next few critical minutes of his life. When he'd lost his mother, he'd thought it would be his last time to have to say goodbye to someone he loved. What a tragic mistake he'd made.

He hooked his thumbs into the belt loops of his blue jeans. "Hal Davis is home. So, uh..." Linc stopped and coughed against his fist. "Anyway, I'll get my things together first thing in the morning. There were a few repairs I hadn't gotten to—"

"Oh, don't worry about it," Jillian stated. "The way I figure it, we're even."

"Yeah—that's right," Linc replied, feeling like an idiot for wanting to pull her into his arms instead of telling her goodbye. He started for the door, but stopped and turned around. "Will you do me one favor?"

Linc saw when Jillian tensed.

"That depends," she replied.

"I'd like to be the one who tells Eric that I'm leaving. The best time, I think, would be after his game tomorrow. Will you let me do that?"

"Why should I?"

Linc stuck his fingertips into the back pockets of his jeans and dropped his gaze to the floor. "No reason."

"Then what difference does it make who tells him?"

He should have known that Jillian would make this so very difficult for him.

"Look, it makes a difference to me," Linc retorted. "Okay?"

Jillian glared at him in a way that suggested it wasn't okay with her. But after a couple of seconds, she cut her eyes toward Eric's school photo that hung on the wall nearby, and sighed heavily. "It'll probably make a difference to Eric, too."

Linc frowned. "What exactly are you saying?"

"I'm saying yes. I'll grant you this one favor." Then she walked to the door and held it open. "But don't make the mistake of asking for another one. We're paid up—even— Mr. Rider. Lock, stock and barrel. Now, good night."

Every muscle in Linc's body tensed. He'd known all along that she was anxious to be rid of him. Why? She'd probably given herself lots of excuses. One, he knew, had to do with her thinking that his way of life was a bad influence on Eric. Well, he didn't want his son to be a drifter, either.

But Jillian had another, much deeper reason for wanting him out of her life. One she would never admit to herself. Passion. Her passion, to be exact. The sleeping tigress that had lain dormant for all these years just beneath the surface of her skin.

Simply put, he'd awakened the woman in her, just as somehow she'd awakened a part of him he'd never known existed. What a pity that the circumstances of their lives had to be as they were. Because, other than being a father to his son, he would have wanted nothing more from this world than to spend the rest of his life loving Jillian as she deserved to be loved. But for him to have his wishes, he'd have to be honest with her and with Eric and take the chance that his surprising revelation to them wouldn't result in creating more emotional harm than good. And frankly, taking that kind of chance with those he loved simply went against his better judgment. Possibly, for the first time in his life, Linc Easy Rider was putting the needs of others before his own. Possibly, for the first time in his life, he was learning what love was really all about.

Linc sauntered up to Jillian and gazed into her eyes. Finally one corner of his mouth lifted in a grin as he cradled the side of her face with his hand. "Has anyone ever told you that you're a beautiful woman?"

He heard her sharp intake of breath. She started to pull away, but then stopped and gazed back at him. "No. Never."

"I find that hard to believe. Still, I'm glad I'm the first."

Then his lips covered hers softly for one long, timeless moment. When he pulled away, tears glistened in his eyes. He turned and quickly vanished into the night without uttering another word.

Jillian shut the door and then stood with her back against it for the longest time. In her dreamlike state, she could still feel the sweet potency of his full mouth on hers. And in that moment, her only wish was to keep that feeling forever.

But, all too soon, she found herself returning to reality and she couldn't lie to herself any longer. If there was one thing Jillian was beginning to understand about herself, it was her need to be loved by a good man. Someone who would make her feel special, even beautiful.

Linc Rider had said she was beautiful. And when he kissed her, she even felt beautiful, too. But she knew he probably said and did that to every *hardy* woman he met. And knowing that he'd be on the move again soon only made her realize that within a couple of days—a week at the most—he'd be saying the same line to someone new.

Now, that thought hurt.

The following morning Jillian was busy with customers from the time she opened. Most of the area farmers usually waited until Saturday mornings when she had extra help to pick up their sacks of field and fertilizer for the coming week. And today was no exception.

Because of the all-star tournament being held at the ballpark, coaches and parents were dropping in for ice and cold drinks. Several people purchased sunscreen and one man bought a wide-brimmed straw hat that Jillian had had on display for a couple of years. As nice as it was to be busy, Jillian silently hoped the flow of traffic would slow down by two o'clock so she could feel comfortable about leaving Gram in charge of the store while she went to Eric's game. Although her mother-in-law's health had rejuvenated itself in the past few days, Jillian was still concerned, especially about the old woman's arthritis.

Linc hadn't come to breakfast that morning, which didn't surprise Jillian any. Eric, however, had become overly concerned. So much so that Jillian had finally allowed him to be excused from the table early, just so he could go in search of his friend. Apparently they'd found each other right away, because the next thing Jillian had known, the two of them were in the backyard, playing catch.

She'd watched them for just a moment, wondering if the attraction she'd felt for Linc didn't have something to do with the wild, unsettling spirit she sensed in him. Not that it mattered one way or the other. He was a drifting soul, all right. And she was a marooned heart. They were opposites. They simply didn't fit together.

In a way Jillian felt kind of sad for Linc. Everyone—whether they wanted to admit it or not—needed a place to call home. But Linc was the type who didn't stay in one spot long enough to allow the engine of his motorcycle to cool down completely. He was constantly leaving behind all the good things in life that would make a lot of warm and wonderful memories for him in his later years. For one thing, he would never know true love, because he would never stick around one place long enough for it to take root and grow. For another, he would never have a home filled with love. Nor a family to count on when times were bad. What a pity.

But if that was the life-style that Linc wanted, then what could she do about it? If his freedom meant more to him than anything, he would never be happy staying in one place all his life. She wouldn't even consider asking him.

Therefore, she wasn't going to spend the rest of her life mourning something that would never be. This was her home. Lord only knew, it wasn't much in the eyes of the world. At times, she almost hated it. She was overworked and underpaid, if, indeed, money was counted as her only reward. But it wasn't, thank God. In the past few days she had begun to realize her many blessings. She was living and loving and making special memories with Eric and Gram that would last her a lifetime. Simply put, she was glad that she belonged here. She only wished that Linc could have found that he did, too....

Just as Eric often did on Saturdays, he offered to make sandwiches for lunch. Gram had just taken Jillian's place behind the checkout counter for a while and Jillian was walking into the kitchen to meet her son when she saw him going out the back door with a brown paper sack clutched tightly in one hand. Her eyes followed him as he raced across the backyard and disappeared inside the outdoor kitchen. Undoubtedly the brown paper sack held a couple of salami sandwiches he had prepared for Linc. But instead of becoming angry with her son, Jillian smiled sadly. Eric was really going to miss Linc.

Jillian ate and then went back into the store to relieve Gram. Soon afterward, Eric, dressed in his all-star uniform, came to meet her.

"What do you think?" Eric said, smiling from ear to ear.

"Oh, Eric, you look fine. Just fine. I'm so proud of you," Jillian replied, giving him a quick hug.

"I hope I don't strike out," he said, and a worried expression suddenly replaced his smile.

"Do the best you can, honey. That's all anyone can ever ask of you."

Looking as though he wasn't quite convinced of his mother's wisdom, Eric nodded and then walked outside to wait for his ride to the game. But after fifteen minutes, he came back inside.

"Mom, Coach says we have to be at the ballpark forty-five minutes to an hour before the game. If Ted's mom doesn't show up soon, we're going to be late. Real late. Coach ain't gonna like it."

Jillian glanced at the clock. "The word to use is *isn't*, Eric." Then in a steady voice, she said, "And Ted's mother still has a few minutes, so—"

The ringing of the telephone interrupted Jillian. She reached for the receiver. "Hello?"

"Jillian, it's Sandra. Listen, I had a flat tire about a half mile from my house. Paula Pitre was passing with a carload of players and she found room for Ted. I'm afraid you'll have to get Eric to the game on your own. I'm sorry."

"Don't worry about it," Jillian replied. "I'll manage." Then once she'd hung up the telephone, she added, "Somehow."

"I'm going to have to find a way to get you to the game, Eric. Ted's mother has a flat tire on her car. Ted got a ride with someone else."

"I'm gonna be the only one late," he cried out.

Jillian was trying to organize her thoughts. She knew that Gram was taking a bath, so her mother-in-law wasn't of any help at the moment. "I'll just close the store for a few minutes," she said.

"Maybe Linc could take me on his motorcycle," Eric replied, his face beaming with color. "That'd be neat."

"No, Eric. You know how I feel about that."

"Aw, Mom. Why not? I've even got a helmet to wear."

Jillian's eyes widened. "Where did you get a helmet?"

"From Barney, Mom. Remember last year when he gave me his old one? Well, I still have it in my closet."

"That's not the point," Jillian was saying as she heard the entrance door squeak open and turned to see Linc walking inside. And as always when he made a sudden appearance, Jillian felt her stomach drop to her knees.

Looking at her son, Jillian said, "Linc doesn't have time to take you to your game. He has other things on his mind." She glanced back at Linc. "Don't you, Linc?"

Linc hesitated for just a second. And then he gave her a cocky smile. "No. As a matter of fact, I don't have other things on my mind. I'll be more than happy to take Eric to his game."

"On your motorcycle?" Eric chimed in as only a highly charged, overexcited eleven-year-old boy would do.

"Yeah, sure. But we'd have to find you a helmet first."

"I have one," Eric said. "It's old, but Barney said it was still good when he gave it to me."

"Then we're all set," Linc said, smiling at Eric.

"Please, Mom," Eric pleaded. "Just this once. I'll never ask again. I promise."

Jillian had faced the fact that she had the tendency to be an overprotective mother. Every once in a while some of the kids at school teased Eric because of it. But, in her case, being overprotective of Eric came with the territory. He was all she had in this world.

"It's too dangerous."

"He'll drive slow," Eric replied. "Won't you, Linc?"

"I can."

Jillian was shaking her head. "But if you wreck—"

"I've never one time ditched a bike in my life. And that's a fact," Linc replied, his voice gruff and to the point.

"Never?" Jillian found herself asking. Her insides were shaking at the thought of Eric on that motorcycle. But she had promised herself to make a change in attitude toward certain situations and she was trying real hard to be fair. Besides, she knew she had to start somewhere. But in her case, letting go of Eric...well...that was a tough place to begin.

"Never," Linc replied. "I'm a good driver. I'm a safe driver. But that's all I can say in my defense. The decision to allow Eric to ride with me is all yours, Jillian."

Jillian was appalled with herself. She was actually thinking of giving in to Eric's wishes. And it had nothing to do with her having to close or not close the store for a while. She'd already resolved that problem in her mind during the night. From now on, when Eric needed her to be with him, and Gram couldn't take over the store for her, she was going to close down. Period. Her son came first. And for having that bit of realization forced upon her, she would always be grateful to Linc.

"All right," Jillian exclaimed. "Just this once."

In his excitement, Eric yelled and then dived toward his mother to give her a big hug, only to pull away seconds later. "Let me get my helmet."

Then Jillian and Linc were left alone.

Chapter Ten

Jillian cleared her throat. She wiped the palms of her hands down the sides of her blue cotton skirt. Only seconds had passed, but already she was having regrets about her decision to allow Eric on that motorcycle. "What if—"

"I'll take extra good care of him, Jillian. So you needn't worry," Linc said, following her with his eyes as she walked behind the checkout counter.

"I can assure you, Linc, that if I didn't believe you meant that wholeheartedly, I wouldn't be letting him go. But it still frightens me to think of what could happen."

One side of Linc's mouth lifted in a lopsided grin. "Of course it does. You're concerned for his safety."

"He's my whole life, Linc," Jillian said, her voice sounding grave. "He's all I've got in this whole world."

Linc's expression suddenly changed. It was as if, for one brief instant, he was able to experience her feelings of dread. "Believe me, Jillian. I know exactly what you mean."

"I'm ready," Eric announced as he rushed back to the front of the store.

Linc immediately spun around and faced him. "Me, too. Did you find the helmet?"

"I got it right here," Eric replied. With his one free hand he grabbed up his baseball glove that he'd left on the counter and hurried outside. Over his shoulder, he said, "Come on, Linc. I'm gonna be late."

"I'm coming, kid," Linc replied, strolling toward the door. Suddenly he stopped and glanced back at Jillian. "You will be at the game, won't you?"

"Yes," Jillian stated breathlessly. "And please be careful. Make sure that Eric puts his helmet on correctly."

For just a moment, Linc's eyes seemed to fill with compassion. "I'll take care of him, Jillian. I promise."

Then he was gone. And within a couple of seconds both Linc and Eric disappeared around the corner of the building and Jillian lost sight of them. A minute later, as she was helping a customer who had just walked in, she heard Linc's motorcycle roar to life.

After that, business slowed down considerably. In fact, the next hour seemed to crawl by. When Gram finally came to take her place, Jillian found herself anxious to go. She slung the strap of her purse over her shoulder and, within minutes, she had Old Yeller heading down the road toward the ballpark.

Upon arriving, Jillian found the parking lot already filled. But when a woman driving a new light blue Buick pulled out just ahead of her, Jillian was able to maneuver Old Yeller into the spot.

She climbed out of the pickup, slammed the door and turned in the direction of the game—and right smack into Barney Langford.

"Hey, Jillian, what's your hurry?" he said.

Jillian placed her hand against Barney's chest in an attempt to ward off his intentions as she continued walking. "I don't have time for this right now, Barney."

"All I want to do is introduce you to my new girlfriend," he said soulfully. "That's all."

Realizing for the first time that someone was indeed following right behind Barney, Jillian halted.

"Hi, Jillian," the woman said, grinning shyly as she stepped around Barney. "It's just me."

Minerva Crenshaw was a young widow with two children. She was also Pine Creek's most holier-than-thou person. She was the head, body and soul of every church committee there was. Minerva Crenshaw and Barney Langford? Together? Who would have ever believed it?

"Uh...I—look, Jillian," Barney stammered. "I just want to say I'm sorry for all the trouble I caused you. I told Minerva what I'd done and she said I owed you an apology."

Jillian watched as Minerva smiled at Barney, and the man actually blushed. "Apology accepted," Jillian replied.

"Now come along, Barney," Minerva said sweetly. "I have a committee meeting in twenty minutes. I hope you haven't forgotten your promise to go with me."

"Why, of course not, honey bun," Jillian heard Barney say as the couple went on their way. She saw Minerva's youngest son run to meet them.

Shaking her head in amused disbelief—talk about opposites attracting—Jillian hurried along. Inside the ballpark she found four games already in progress. It took a minute to recognize Eric's team, but once she did, she walked over and took a seat at the top of the bleachers. Searching the crowd, she immediately saw Linc standing at the chain-link fence that surrounded the diamond. He was wearing a baseball cap and Jillian almost didn't recognize him.

The umpire behind home plate got everyone's attention when he announced in a loud voice, "Batter up."

Jillian saw Eric sitting in the dugout with his team, and she waved to him. When she glanced back in Linc's direction, she saw him searching the crowd, and from the change in his expression, she knew he'd spotted her. Then he turned around and continued watching the ball game.

By the close of the first inning, the score was tied zero to zero. The day was clear and warm and, for Jillian, it felt wonderful to be outdoors on a sunny Saturday afternoon as though she had nothing in the world better to do. She felt alive.

Or at least, she was feeling good until she noticed Wilma Jenkins sashay herself right up to Linc. It was incredible how, in that one moment, all of Jillian's good feelings were so easily flushed from her body.

Wilma said something to Linc and he threw back his head and laughed. A wave of jealousy knifed through Jillian and she felt sick to her stomach. She deliberately turned her head, promising herself that she wouldn't look back at them again. Linc's choice in the women he enjoyed was none of her business.

Not that she cared—really.

Actually, she didn't care if the two of them lived happily ever after.

Liar.

Jillian forced herself to concentrate solely on Eric's game. A couple of minutes later, she felt someone tugging at her elbow, glanced down and saw that Linc was standing there, gazing up at her.

"Can I get you something to drink?" he asked.

Jillian glanced toward the fence and saw that Wilma was still standing in the same spot, only now she was peering at Jillian with a frown on her face.

"A cola would be nice."

Linc went to the concession stand for their drinks. He was back in less than five minutes and handed her two tall paper cups filled with ice and soda. Then he hiked up his leg on one of the bleachers near her, pulled himself up and sat down. Jillian cut her eyes back to where Wilma stood, only to discover that the woman had vanished.

"Where's Wilma?" Jillian asked.

Linc glanced at her. "How would I know? I'm not Wilma's keeper."

"I just thought—"

"I know what you thought," Linc said, cutting her off. He was looking straight ahead at the game. "But you're wrong. Now, drink up before your ice melts."

The momentum in Eric's game picked up and by the bottom of the seventh and last inning, Jillian's throat hurt from all the cheering she'd done on his team's behalf. By now, she'd eaten too much popcorn and drank at least one too many sodas. Her skin was turning pink from her being out in the sun for so long a period. She felt stuffed, dusty and tired. And she was having the time of her life.

Eric's team was one run behind their opponent. By the time it was Eric's turn to bat, two players on his team had already been called out. The overall tension of the game had been building to this moment and, as a result, the crowd of parents and spectators was extremely rambunctious. Ignoring the fact that they weren't the team's coach, several parents—mostly fathers—walked up to the fence behind home plate and began yelling instructions to Eric. Jillian could tell from the expression on her son's face that he was already a nervous wreck. Jillian wished there were something she could do for him. But short of taking his place in the batter's box, there wasn't anything she could do. Seeking comfort, she reached for Linc's hand. "He's scared to death," she whispered.

Giving a deep sigh, Linc squeezed her hand. "I know. I can tell." Then, in a lowered voice, he said, "I wish those bastards would shut up."

"Me, too," Jillian replied.

The pitcher threw the first ball and Eric swung at it and missed. The crowd groaned. Jillian felt as though her heart were going to pound through her chest. She squeezed Linc's hand even tighter. Dear God, let him hit the next one.

A second pitch was thrown, this one too high, but Eric swung at it anyway. This time, the majority of the crowd stood and roared in protest. Jillian shut her eyes tight.

Suddenly, Linc tore his hand from hers and jumped to the ground. He marched to the chain-link fence just behind home plate—where all those fathers were standing—and grabbed hold of it with his hands. Even though he spoke in a calm, clear voice, Jillian had to strain against all the noise to hear what he was saying.

"Don't pay these people any mind, Eric. Just listen to your coach, watch for his signals and keep your eye on the ball when you swing."

Then Linc backed off from the fence as Eric prepared for the third and—perhaps—final pitch. When Eric swung his bat and made the connection that sent the ball sailing over second base, Linc shouted, "Run, Eric." Jillian jumped up and clapped her hands while tears of joy sprang to her eyes. By some miracle, Eric hadn't struck out. And then he was called safe at first base. Thank goodness.

The next batter stepped up and on his first pitch sent the ball flying over the fence at center field. It was a home run with three men on base. Eric's team went ahead to win the game and the player who had hit the homer was declared a hero.

After the excitement wore down, Eric ran to where Linc and Jillian stood, waiting for him. "I didn't strike out," he said breathlessly. "Did you see that, Linc? Mom? I didn't strike out."

"I saw, Eric," Jillian said laughingly. "And I saw your ball sail over second base."

Eric beamed with pride. He faced Linc. "Thanks—for what you said to me."

"I thought you might've needed to hear a friendly voice in the crowd," Linc said with a pleased grin, placing his arm across Eric's shoulders and giving him a hard, fast hug.

"Are we going for pizza like you said?" Eric asked.

"Yes, indeed," Linc replied. "A promise is a promise. I said that if you played your very best, I'd buy you a pizza. You gave it your best shot, and I'm very proud of you, son."

Eric grinned. "Thanks, Linc."

Linc peered at Jillian. "Would you like to join us for pizza?"

"I—I can't," Jillian stammered. "I have to get back to the store. I'm sure Gram is anxious for me to return."

"We shouldn't be more than a couple of hours," Linc stated. "I think some of the other kids from his team are going, too."

"I can't go," Jillian replied. "But—"

"I'll take care of Eric," Linc said.

"You will be careful?" Jillian asked.

"Yes."

"Come on, Linc," Eric stated, tugging at his arm. "'Bye, Mom. See you later."

Linc's eyes drilled into hers. "'Bye, Jillian."

"Goodbye," she replied. And that was when she realized she wasn't ever going to see him again. This was it. He was walking away from her as if it were nothing. And later, he'd walk away from Eric in the same fashion. Without experiencing one single regret. That hurt.

For Linc, turning his back on Jillian and walking away without a backward glance was the hardest thing he'd ever had to do in his life. And he knew that his pain wasn't nearly over yet. In fact, it was just beginning. Soon he'd have to do the same thing to his own son. His heart felt as though it were being ripped from his body. It wasn't fair. It simply wasn't fair.

Better for you to suffer than for him, Linc's inner voice said. And for once, since learning he had a son, he and his inner voice were in total agreement.

Linc and Eric rode the fifteen miles to join his teammates for pizza. But within an hour's time, they were the only two who remained. And Linc knew the time he dreaded most had come at last.

"Eric, I have something to tell you."

Eric stopped moving in his seat and leveled his gaze on Linc's face. "What?"

"You remember the agreement between your mother and me? I was to work for her until my friend came home from Florida?" Linc waited for Eric to nod in agreement. "Well, my friend has come back. So now—"

"You're leaving," Eric interrupted. "Aren't you?"

Linc felt his heart swell up. "Yes, I'm leaving, but please... let me explain."

Eric looked off in another direction. "You don't have to explain nothing to me," he said. "I understand."

"Eric, look at me," Linc said. "Please. I know you're disappointed—"

Eric cut his eyes back to Linc. "You don't know nothing about me. And you don't care, either. I thought you liked it here. I thought you were my friend. I thought... I thought..." Suddenly, Eric's eyes were filled with tears.

"I am your friend, Eric. And I'll always be your friend."

Eric sniffed. "Are you coming back?"

Linc felt that someone was twisting a knife in his heart. "No. At least, not for a long time." He leaned across the table and took Eric by the shoulders, forcing his son to look at him. "But I'll always be your friend. Always. Here," Linc continued as he reached inside his shirt pocket and pulled out a slip of paper. "This is for you. It's the tele-

phone number and street address of some people whom I've
known for a long time. They're my friends and they always
know how to find me. If you ever need anything—or if your
mother ever needs anything—anything at all, you call
them."

"But why can't you just stay with us?" Eric asked.

"I can't, Eric. There are circumstances that you don't
understand. I have to go," Linc replied. "It wouldn't be
right for me to stay."

"I don't understand," Eric said, hanging his head.

Linc sighed heavily. "Sometimes, neither do I, kid."

"When are you leaving?"

"Tonight."

Again, Eric looked away. "Oh."

Linc drew in a steadying breath. "Keep that paper I just
gave you in a safe place. And it's best if you don't give out
the information on it to anyone. Not even your mother. She
might not like it."

"Will you write me?"

"I'm not much on writing letters, kid. But I guess it won't
hurt anything if I drop you a postcard from time to time."

Eric's face brightened. He almost smiled. "Will you ever
come back?"

Linc's smile was bittersweet. "Maybe someday. Now, I'd
better get you home. Your mama's going to be worried if
we're late."

The ride back to Pine Creek was the shortest journey Linc
had ever taken. To him, it seemed that he and Eric had just
climbed on his Harley and now they were home.

It was too soon.

He wasn't ready to let go of Eric.

He would never be ready to let go of Eric.

But he would do it, because he was now convinced that it
was the best thing he could do for his son.

"Goodbye, Linc," Eric was saying, his hand outstretched in front of him.

Linc took Eric's hand, but it wasn't enough. Suddenly, he wrapped his arms around Eric's shoulders and hugged him. And for just a moment, Linc's eyes filled with tears.

"Goodbye, kid. Stay out of trouble. And take care of your mama. And always remember, you know where to find me." Then, after making sure his duffel bag was still secure, he gunned the motor of his Harley and shot out of there as fast as he could.

Linc had been gone for three days now, and for the most part, Jillian's days had fallen into the same old routine as before. She'd thought that Eric would have wanted to talk to her about Linc, but other than a few remarks on the first day, he hadn't mentioned the man's name. This afternoon, he had gone swimming with a friend. Jillian felt that was a good sign that he was feeling better.

But, unfortunately, she wasn't. In the past three days her thoughts had been filled with Linc. Where was he? What was he doing? Had he found someone else to give his kisses to?

She could hardly stand thinking about that last one.

Without Linc's presence, everything seemed so normal again. So ordinary. During those few, wonderful days that he'd been in her life, she'd experienced a sweet anticipation that had made her feel alive. Now that he was gone, she could so easily admit that to herself. Why hadn't she recognized it before now?

She missed him. She missed his voice—his heated glances—his silly smiles. And...yes...yes...*yes*...she missed his kisses.

All the sanctimonious lectures she'd given herself about who not to fall in love with had all been for nothing. She loved Linc Rider. And she wanted him back. But he was the one who had left her, and she wasn't about to go begging after any man.

Her telephone started ringing. Frowning, she glanced at it with a sense of irritation. Already twice that day she'd hurried to answer the phone, and on both occasions the caller had hesitated for just a moment and then had hung up.

Jillian lifted the receiver. "Hello?" When the caller hesitated, Jillian repeated herself. "Hello? Who is this?"

"My name isn't important."

Jillian was stunned that someone—a woman, she thought—had actually spoken. "You've reached Fontenot's Grocery. Is there something I can do for you?"

"Please...you must be patient. This...this isn't easy for me. I've tried calling before, b-but I always lost my nerve to speak to you. This is Mrs. Henry Fontenot, isn't it?"

Hardly anyone ever referred to Jillian in that fashion anymore. "Yes...yes, it is." Jillian strained to hear what was going on at the other end of the line. She wasn't sure if the woman was sickly, or crying, or what.

"I feel I must warn you."

Jillian was leaning against the counter, but stood up straight. "What do you mean? Warn me about what? Who is this?"

"Please," the woman pleaded. "You must believe me. Your son could be in danger."

"My son?" Jillian responded. "What does my son have to do with this?"

Now Jillian was certain that the woman was crying. "I made a terrible mistake," the caller declared. "Please...you must forgive me. I meant you no harm. I thought... Look, I had no idea that he would react the way he did to the news."

Jillian could feel her apprehension mounting. "What news? Please, *who is this?*"

The woman sniffed for a few moments before she began to speak again. "I didn't think there would be any harm in telling him about the baby. Not after all these years. But I was wrong."

Jillian felt the wind go out of her. When she spoke, it was in a grave voice. "What exactly are you telling me?"

"Your son's natural father isn't dead. I know you thought he was, but he isn't."

Jillian's insides squeezed together. Her hands began to tremble. "Eric is legally mine."

"I know that. But he wants the boy. He told me himself that he would do anything to get him. Last I heard, he'd gotten himself a private investigator. I think Easy means business. I do feel that he could be dangerous."

Jillian couldn't breathe. Her body simply refused to take in the oxygen she needed to survive. Finally, after what seemed an eternity, she managed to suck in enough air to keep her going. "Easy? Did you say, *Easy?*"

"Easy Rider. That's what everyone called him back then."

Jillian's heart was pounding. "What does he look like?"

"Dark hair...and...and blue eyes."

Jillian felt the blood draining from her face. Her head suddenly felt light. But surely she wasn't going to faint again. "Do you think he would be capable of kidnapping my son?"

"Yes, I think he could be."

"Oh, God..." Jillian replied.

"Look, I—I wanted to warn you," the woman was saying. "I felt I owed you that much. But I don't want to be involved in anything, hear? My daughter doesn't know about this call. She'd be upset with me if she did. I'll deny everything if you get me caught up in the middle."

"I have no reason to do that," Jillian replied.

"The boy. Is he all right?" the woman asked nervously.

"Yes," Jillian replied, feeling as though she was in a state of shock. Surely this couldn't be happening.

Without another word, the woman hung up. After a few moments Jillian replaced the receiver and just stood there, trying to gather her thoughts.

It couldn't be true. Could it?

A sudden panic seized hold of her. Oh, dear God, but where was Eric? She ran to the back and found him sound asleep on the floor in front of the television, all safe and sound. Thank goodness.

Her insides were in shambles. So many crazy thoughts were racing through her mind, she couldn't even think straight. Was Linc the person the woman had described? Or rather, was he the *kind* of person the woman had described? Finally, one thought was persistent enough to take root and, like Jack's beanstalk, shoot up high above all the others.

Linc Rider was Eric's biological father.

It had to be true. It even made sense—to some degree. She'd just been too blinded by her attraction to him to see what was right there under her nose.

And he'd come to Pine Creek for one purpose.

Eric.

Frightened by that knowledge, Jillian shivered. What a little fool she'd been.

What had he hoped to accomplish by coming here? Surely he had known that Eric was legally and morally and in every way her son, and that she would never, *ever* give him up. Not for any reason.

God forbid! Would he have kidnapped Eric if he had had the opportunity?

But she had given him the opportunity. Several times. So why hadn't he?

Perhaps he still planned to. Maybe he was coming back for Eric.

For the remainder of the day, Jillian's emotions went from anger to hurt to fear. The hurt came from realizing what a fool she'd been. She kept thinking of that day at Eric's game and the way she and Linc had held hands in comfort. What a fake he was. She thought of the way he'd taken care of her on the day of the thunderstorm. And his kisses. She couldn't stop the memory of his kisses. What was he up to now? Did he plan to come back like a thief in the night and kidnap her son from her? It hurt to think that she could so easily have fallen in love with someone capable of such a hideous crime.

The whole thing seemed so bizarre. Yet, at the same time, the more she thought about everything, the more she saw all the little signs she had missed.

It all fit together. No matter how crazy it seemed, it all fit together. Linc was Eric's father.

The thought was bittersweet.

It hurt. It made her cry. It made her want to seek answers. For her own peace of mind.

Jillian knew the moment when she began heading into real trouble. It was just about the time she realized that she still loved Linc in spite of everything. Maybe because of the fact that he *was* Eric's father. She just didn't know anymore. But deep down inside, she knew that some part of her still trusted that Linc wouldn't have harmed them. Nor would he do so now. The other part of her said she was a fool.

That was why she had to find out the truth.

Later that night, when she came from the bathroom after a long, hot soak, Jillian noticed that Eric was lying on his stomach across his bed and was staring out the window into the night. He didn't seem to hear her as she stepped inside his room. "What's wrong, Eric?"

"Nothing," he said without looking at her.

"Are you sure?" Jillian asked, moving to his bed and sitting on the edge of it. She ran her fingers through his disheveled hair. "A lot has happened lately."

"I was just thinking," he said.

"About what?" Jillian asked, smiling down at him. God...if she ever lost him...if ever he were taken from her...

Eric continued staring out the window. "About Linc."

Jillian felt herself stiffen.

Eric flipped over onto his back. "I miss him, Mom. I guess I shouldn't. But I do. He was my friend."

"Eric," Jillian said, clasping her hand over one of his, "I know he was your friend. But there are a lot of things that you don't know—that I didn't even know—about him."

"That's what he said, too. That there were circumstances that I didn't understand."

Jillian frowned. "When did he tell you all this?"

"On the night he left. While we were eating pizza. He said he had to go, but that he would always be my friend."

Once again, Jillian felt her heart begin to pound. "What else did he tell you, Eric?"

Eric shrugged. "Just stuff."

"What kind of...stuff? It's important that I know."

"I don't know," Eric replied. "Stuff like...don't get into trouble. Take care of your mama."

"He said that?" Jillian asked, feeling a quickening in her pulse.

"Yeah. And I don't care if you believe me or not, but I know he's always going to be my friend."

"I know you believe that, Eric. But—"

"But it's true," Eric said, sitting up. "And I'll prove it to you." He jumped from the bed, opened the bottom drawer of his dresser and began removing his socks and underwear. When he stood up, he held a small piece of paper. "See?" he said, handing it to his mother. "He gave me this address and phone number and said for me to call him if ever I needed anything. Now doesn't that make him sound like he's my friend?''

Jillian stared at the paper she held. There it was. Her one and only chance of ever having total peace of mind ever again. She quickly memorized the name, address and phone number on the paper. Then she handed it back to her son.

"See, Mom, I told you he was my friend."

Jillian took a deep breath and smiled sadly. "Maybe I was wrong about him, son."

"You sure were," Eric replied.

Later that night, Jillian decided Gram needed to be told the truth about Linc Rider. She took the news much better than Jillian expected.

"I sensed something about him all along," Gram said. "But I couldn't quite put my finger on it. But in spite of it all, I found I liked him." She looked seriously at Jillian. "You did, too."

Jillian nodded.

"I think you should go to Biloxi, find him and confront him with everything you know," Gram said. "Eric and I can take care of the store while you're gone."

"I think you're right. I think it's the only way, Gram. At least, the only way for me to ever find peace again. I don't want to have to live looking over my shoulder, constantly wondering if Eric is safe."

"Then do what you have to do, child. You have my blessings."

Jillian didn't want to leave Gram and Eric totally alone in the store. She hired the same high school boy who worked on Saturday mornings to help out until she returned.

By ten o'clock the next morning, she was on her way to Biloxi, Mississippi. She didn't have any idea what she was going to find once she got there. But as sensitive and as vulnerable as she felt, she knew one thing. She *had* to confront Linc. She had to put her mind—and heart—to rest once and for all.

Because hearing the truth from him would set her free.

She had to believe that.

Linc was miserable. He wanted so much to talk to Jillian, to explain everything to her and to have her know and understand his motive for what he'd done. But it was no use. He'd lied to her. He'd used her. She would never believe his love for her was real. She'd think it was another one of his schemes. And he couldn't blame her.

He missed his son. God, it was awful the way he missed the boy.

He'd made the biggest mistake of his life, thinking that he could just walk in on his son's life and whisk him away from all he'd ever known without any complications. And the second biggest mistake of his life was underestimating his own vulnerability.

But how could he have ever guessed that he would fall in love with his son's adoptive mother? And who would have ever guessed that his love for both of them would be his reason for walking away?

Well, at least he had the knowledge that he had done the right thing for them. But, unfortunately for him, that knowledge didn't mend his broken heart.

His old landlord had given him back his one-room apartment without asking too many questions. It had taken Linc all of five minutes to unpack and settle in. The first thing he'd done was visit an attorney's office. Now Eric was his sole beneficiary if something should ever happen to him.

Opening a beer, he took a deep breath. Now there was nothing more he could do but to get on with his own life. Eric was safe and loved, which was a comfort to know. Jillian, as vulnerable as she was at times, was a fighter and he knew she would be okay, too. Maybe someday she'd find that honest, hard-working man of her dreams. He hoped so. She deserved happiness more than any person he knew. Still, the thought of her with another man ripped a hole in his gut the size of a grapefruit.

Linc heard a soft knock, but he thought it was at the apartment next door to him. He took a sip of his beer and forced his concentration on the late-afternoon news that was on television. His Salisbury steak TV dinner was heating in the oven.

Tomorrow would be five days since he'd last seen them. Five days out of a possible lifetime. He sure as hell had a long way to go.

Linc heard the knock again. Only this time it was louder and more persistent. He stood up, walked to the door and opened it.

"Hello, Linc."

He just gaped at her, his eyes absorbing her every feature.

"May I come inside?" she asked politely.

Dumbfounded, he looked past her. "How did you get here?"

"Old Yeller."

"You mean to tell me you drove that ornery old truck all the way over here by yourself?"

"Yeller's not ornery. Not when you handle him just right. Someone who claimed to be pretty good with vehicles once told me that it was all in the touch. I thought it was pretty good advice."

"Fool advice, if you ask me," Linc said gruffly, stepping aside for Jillian to come in. Just the sight of her face made his heart feel as big as a morning sun. He sucked in a deep breath, filling his nostrils with her sweet, floral scent. His love for her was going to be the death of him yet.

Jillian walked to the center of the room and then turned around to face Linc. Standing with his feet apart, Linc folded his arms and studied her.

"How did you find me?"

"What's the matter, Linc? Does it bother you to know that you're not quite as elusive as you thought you were?"

"Is Eric okay?" he asked anxiously.

"Yes. *My* son is fine."

Linc knew he had to get her out of his place before he exploded into a thousand little pieces. "Then why are you here? You didn't seem like the kind of woman who would go chasing after a man when he's made it obvious he isn't interested."

Jillian stiffened. Those gorgeous blue eyes of his were like razors, cutting her to the bone. "I'm here for the truth. You may not owe me anything else, but after barging into my life—and Eric's, too—you owe me the truth."

Linc shifted his gaze to the television, but he didn't really see the picture on the screen. His eyes went back to her face. She was standing stone still, with the strap of her shoulder bag held tightly in her grip. She looked ready to run. But the lady, he knew, was made of tough stuff. She was here for answers, and Linc had a feeling she wasn't leaving until she got them. "Which is?"

"Why did you come to Pine Creek in the first place? And don't give me the cock-and-bull story about your friend Hal Davis. I just spoke to Hal Davis ten minutes ago. He lives just down the street from here."

Linc sighed heavily. Then he walked up to Jillian and removed the strap of her purse from her shoulder. "Sit down, Jillian." She quickly did as he wanted. That was when Linc noticed that she was shaking. "Are you cold?"

"No."

"Can I get you something?"

"No."

He sat down beside her.

Squaring her shoulders, Jillian sat erect. "Just tell me the truth, for once," she said without looking at him.

"The truth," Linc repeated. "What good will it do either of us? Just let it be."

"I can't. I can't just let it be. You pushed your way into our lives and...and everything changed. Eric...Gram...me. In fact, the whole world seemed to change. I tried to keep you away. But you didn't stop until you had us believing in you. And then you stole that faith away, right out from under us. I want to know why you did that to us."

Linc thought he'd been suffering. But hearing the anguish in Jillian's voice was like a death sentence. And he deserved it, by God. He damned well deserved it.

"I'm so sorry," he said. "I made a terrible mistake."

Jillian was shaking her head. "That's not good enough anymore. I want to know *why*."

Linc sat back on the sofa and closed his eyes. He had once told her that the piper always had to be paid. He just hadn't realized that he'd be doing the paying and just how high the price would be.

"I've already caused enough pain. Why make it worse?"

"Because you started this. Now I'm here to finish it. And the only way I'll ever have peace of mind is to hear the truth from you."

Linc was silent for a long time. Like a fool, he realized he'd started something that was no longer in his control. And Jillian was right. The only way to stop it was to tell her the truth.

"Eric's my son," he said flatly, thinking how strange it felt to actually be saying it out loud. Knowing that Jillian was probably in shock, he turned his head and gazed at her.

"I know," she replied softly.

Linc felt the wind go out of him. He caught Jillian by the shoulders and turned her so they faced each other. "How did you find out?"

"An anonymous call from a woman who said she'd made a big mistake in telling you that you had a son."

"Mrs. Mcguire."

"She wouldn't give me her name. She said she wanted to warn me about you. She said that you were dangerous." Linc saw when Jillian's eyes filled with tears. "And she was right."

"Oh, God…" he said, wrapping his arms around her and crushing her against him. "I'm sorry I hurt either of you. I love both you and Eric too much."

Jillian pulled away. "I know you love Eric. But don't say you love me. We both know why you came to Pine Creek. And it had nothing to do with me."

Linc held her shoulders and forced her to look at him. "You're right. My arrival at Pine Creek had nothing to do with you. I went there with the sole intention of taking Eric away from you. My plan was to win him over and then to convince him to go away with me. But after seeing the two of you together—after seeing the way you looked after him and loved him—I knew I wouldn't be able to pull if off. And then I fell in love with you and everything got crazy. I knew you would think that I was just using you if I told you the truth. And to tell Eric that I was his father to fill my own needs just didn't seem right anymore. Eric needs you—more than he needs me. I realized I couldn't do it. So I left."

Jillian's heart was racing. "And you weren't planning to come back for Eric?"

"No."

Maybe she was a fool, Jillian thought. But she believed him. Maybe it was the pain she saw deep in his eyes. "I've done a lot of thinking in the past couple of days. I realized that you had plenty of opportunity to tell Eric who you were. You even had the opportunity to take him away." She paused to take a deep breath. Her hand trembled as she smoothed back her hair from her face. "I've thought about the way you took care of me when I got hurt. And...and..."

Linc pulled her back into his arms and whispered, "I thought about you so much that I ached with wanting to hold you." He kissed her lightly on the side of the head. "Ah...sweet Jillian, what a fine mess I've made of everything. I only wish I could have another chance."

"What if I told you that I came to hear the truth from you and then to offer you another chance?" Jillian asked. This time she pulled back to look into his eyes. Those blue, blue eyes that she wanted to believe in so much.

"After all I've done and intended to do, why would you even want to?" he asked.

"Because you're Eric's father, and he needs a father. And because, in spite of everything that's happened, I still love you with all my heart."

Linc felt his own heart skip a beat. "Jillian, if you give me a chance, I promise I'll love you and Eric, and I'll take care of you and him until my dying day."

Lifting her face to his, Jillian smiled her answer. Linc didn't hesitate when he saw the most powerful love he'd ever known shining in her eyes. He covered her mouth in a long, deep kiss that told her everything she would ever need to know about him. And then he said it out loud. "I love you, Jillian."

"I love you, too, Linc."

"But what will Eric think about this—about us?" Linc asked. "I don't want him to be hurt. Not ever. But especially not because of me. I've already caused enough damage and—"

Jillian placed her fingertips over Linc's mouth. "Don't worry about Eric. He's crazy about you. We'll just have to take it slowly with him, one day at a time. But we owe him the truth, and together we'll tell him," Jillian replied.

Linc took a deep, relaxing breath. "And Gram?"

Jillian smiled. "She likes you, Linc. I think she'll be very happy for us."

Linc smiled. "I hope so."

"So. . . can we go home now?" Jillian asked.

"All I need is five minutes to pack. But I'm going to love you for the rest of my life," Linc replied, easing her closer to him. "And I'm going to show you just how much every chance I get."

Jillian's laugh sounded deep in her throat. "You're such a rebel, Linc. Whatever will I do with you?"

Smiling wickedly, Linc's eyes answered her—words weren't necessary. Then, once again, he took her lips with his, and in that moment, they both knew that the sweetness they had found would be theirs forever more.

It was almost midnight by the time Linc and Jillian were ready to return to Pine Creek. Jillian, in her new state of bliss, became adventurous and decided she wanted to ride back with Linc on his Harley. Delighted, Linc made arrangements with a friend for Old Yeller to be driven back to Louisiana in a couple of days.

By the time they arrived home, the sun was already up. Jillian, feeling windblown but deliriously happy, watched as Linc parked his Harley alongside the outdoor kitchen, just as he'd done before. Then Linc swept her into his arms and kissed her long and hard. When they heard the back door to the house open, they pulled apart slowly and turned to see who it was. Linc slipped his arm around Jillian's waist.

"Linc! You've come back," Eric called out excitedly the moment he saw them.

Jillian smiled at her son. Then she rested her head on Linc's shoulder. "Yes, Eric, he's come home. And this time he's here's to stay."

"No kidding!" Eric replied as a smile brightened up his face.

Jillian lifted her head and looked into the deep blue eyes of the man she loved. *Her son had those same blue eyes.* She smiled at him.

And then together, side by side, with hands and hearts and souls joined as one, Linc and Jillian walked forward to greet their son.

*   *   *   *   *

HE'S MORE THAN
A MAN, HE'S
ONE OF OUR

Fabulous Fathers

THE BIRDS AND THE BEES
by Liz Ireland

Bachelor Kyle Weston was going crazy—why else would he be
daydreaming about marriage and children? At first he thought it was
beautiful Mary Moore—and the attraction that still lingered twelve years
after their brief love affair. Then Mary's daughter dropped a bombshell that
shocked Kyle's socks off. Could it be young Maggie Moore was *his* child?
Suddenly fatherhood was more than just a fantasy....

Join in the love—and the laughter—
in Liz Ireland's *THE BIRDS AND THE BEES,*
available in February.

Fall in love with our FABULOUS FATHERS!

Silhouette
R O M A N C E™

Take 4 bestselling love stories FREE

Plus get a FREE surprise gift!

He staked his claim…

HONOR BOUND

by
New York Times
Bestselling Author

Sandra Brown

previously published under the pseudonym Erin St. Claire

As Aislinn Andrews opened her mouth to scream, a hard
hand clamped over her face and she found herself face-
to-face with Lucas Greywolf, a lean, lethal-looking
Navajo and escaped convict who swore he wouldn't hurt
her— *if* she helped him.

Look for HONOR BOUND at your favorite
retail outlet this January.

Only from…

**And now for
something completely different
from Silhouette....**

Unique and innovative stories that take you into the world of paranormal happenings. Look for our special "Spellbound" flash—and get ready for a truly exciting reading experience!

**In February, look for
One Unbelievable Man (SR #993)
by Pat Montana.**

Was he man or myth? Cass Kohlmann's mysterious traveling companion, Michael O'Shea, had her all confused. He'd suddenly appeared, claiming she was his destiny—determined to win her heart. But could levelheaded Cass learn to believe in fairy tales...before her fantasy man disappeared forever?

Don't miss the charming, sexy and utterly mysterious
Michael O'Shea in
ONE UNBELIEVABLE MAN.
Watch for him in February—only from

As seen on TV!
Free Gift Offer

With a Free Gift proof-of-purchase from any Silhouette® book, you can receive a beautiful cubic zirconia pendant.

This gorgeous marquise-shaped stone is a genuine cubic zirconia—accented by an 18" gold tone necklace.

(Approximate retail value $19.95)

Send for yours today...
compliments of ▼ *Silhouette*®

To receive your free gift, a cubic zirconia pendant, send us one original proof-of-purchase, photocopies not accepted, from the back of any Silhouette Romance™, Silhouette Desire®, Silhouette Special Edition®, Silhouette Intimate Moments® or Silhouette Shadows™ title for January, February or March 1994 at your favorite retail outlet, together with the Free Gift Certificate, plus a check or money order for $2.50 (do not send cash) to cover postage and handling, payable to Silhouette Free Gift Offer. We will send you the specified gift. Allow 6 to 8 weeks for delivery. Offer good until March 31st, 1994 or while quantities last. Offer valid in the U.S. and Canada only.

Free Gift Certificate

Name: _____

Address: _____

City: _____ State/Province: _____ Zip/Postal Code: _____

Mail this certificate, one proof-of-purchase and a check or money order for postage and handling to: SILHOUETTE FREE GIFT OFFER 1994. In the U.S.: 3010 Walden Avenue, P.O. Box 9057, Buffalo NY 14269-9057. In Canada: P.O. Box 622, Fort Erie, Ontario L2Z 5X3

FREE GIFT OFFER
079-KBZ

ONE PROOF-OF-PURCHASE

To collect your fabulous FREE GIFT, a cubic zirconia pendant, you must include this original proof-of-purchase for each gift with the properly completed Free Gift Certificate.

079-KBZ